London Spirits
Short Stories

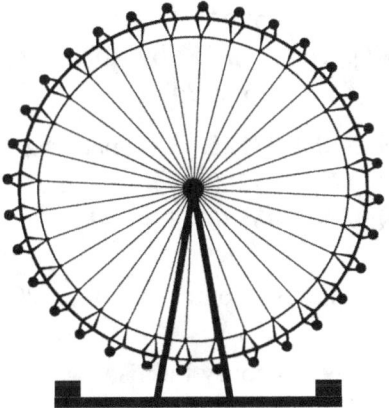

Rob Burton

STANSBURY
PUBLISHING
Chico, Ca.

LONDON SPIRITS
Short Stories
Copyright © 2017 by Rob Burton
First Edition

ISBN: 978-1-935807-33-9 paperback
ISBN: 978-1-935807-34-6 Kindle
ISBN: 978-1-935807-35-3 ePub

Library of Congress Control Number: 2017953380

Stansbury Publishing
An Imprint of Heidelberg Graphics
2 Stansbury Court
Chico, California 95928

Dedicated to those

who are no longer with us

but still remain close by.

□□□□□

Contents

PART ONE: NOW

□□□□□

The Knowledge

"Do you want to know a secret?" the man asks. I look around the pub, slightly bemused by the question.

"Well, do you?" he insists. He glares at me as if his life depends on an immediate answer.

I put my smartphone down and smile vaguely in his direction.

He moves closer to me. "There are ghosts beneath us," he says. "I mean real ghosts. At least two of them."

"Really?" I say, casually. I take a sip of beer and again check to see if other customers are listening. But they seem engrossed in their own private conversations.

The man continues. "Yes, I know all about them, you see. They've been walking the cellars for over a hundred years. Such a sad story."

He swills his beer and studies the foam slide down the side of his glass as if it's some kind of living organism. Then he drains it quickly and burps.

"Fancy another pint, then?" he says, cheerily all of a sudden. "Go on, it will do you good."

Seeing that it's raining cats and dogs outside and the pub feels warm and cozy, I agree. Besides, I've got no immediate plans for the afternoon, having spent most of the morning at the National Tate Gallery around the corner, admiring the paintings of J. M. W. Turner. Perhaps my new friend might provide a welcome distraction from the breaking story of the day: the black cab protest against Uber, the American ride-sharing service, which had brought most of central London's transportation system to a standstill and which forced me to make the two-mile hike from my hotel to the Tate in the slashing rain. Standing there in the gallery, wet and miserable, I was able to appreciate once again how the paintings of Turner speak to a fundamental part of the British psyche. In a climate of seemingly endless dampness and grey skies, his bold experiments in light and color offer a timely reminder that the sun does occasionally make an appearance in these parts. I should know; I was British once. I grew up in the damp and drizzle. That was over thirty years ago, before I moved to the sunny climes of California and became an American.

The man takes both empty glasses to the bar and places his order. He is short and stocky, dressed in black cotton trousers and a bright blue V-necked sweater which contrasts with his chubby red face. He seems to enjoy a joke with the bartender who, after pouring the drinks, offers a mock salute as if he's addressing Lord Horatio Nelson or the like.

He comes back to the table and burps again, without an apology. "Here we go! Two pints of London Pride. Cheers, mate!"

I clink glasses and reach for my phone.

"Are you married to that bloody thing?" he says, wagging his finger at my digital device.

"Sorry," I say. "I was getting the latest news about the taxi strike."

"Ay, yes. It's a crying shame, ain't it? A bloody mess, if you ask me. Still, I can't say that I blame the cab drivers though. They've got a point to prove, haven't they?"

"To be honest, I haven't studied the issue that deeply," I say. "I'm not totally sure why they're on strike. All I know is that I had to walk here today from my hotel. It wasn't much fun in the rain."

"Can't be helped, mate," he shrugs. "You see, it's all about the Knowledge," he says in a hushed voice as if he's sharing some kind of state secret.

I take a mouthful of beer and glance at the picture of a half-naked woman on the wall.

"Oh yes, and that's Mata Hari," he says approvingly. "Quite a looker, eh? The most beautiful spy of all time." He studies her for a few seconds. "This place is crawling with them, you know."

"What! Lookers, you mean?"

"No, you daft bugger. Spies. See that building over there?" He nods in the direction of the window and points to a grey structure on the far side of the River Thames that looks like it belongs to Legoland. "That's where they work. The MI6 building. Home of British Intelligence. The agents come here often for lunch and a pint. You can tell who they are by the black ties, starched shirts, and single-breasted suits."

"Not forgetting the George Smiley glasses and James Bond haircut," I say.

"It's no laughing matter, mate." He gets closer to my face, lowering his voice. "Just be careful what you say around here, that's all. You never know who's listening, or who's watching, for that matter."

He looks around, burps, and smiles at the smartly-dressed couple at the next table who are clearly unsettled by my friend's behavior. Then he resumes his normal voice.

"Anyhow, as I was saying, you've got to feel sorry for the London cabbies," he says. "They work bloody hard to acquire the Knowledge. It can take them up to three years to memorize all the streets in central London, not to mention every single landmark over an area of about a hundred square miles. At the end of it all, they earn the famous Green Badge. It doesn't come cheaply, that's for sure."

"Yes, that's all very commendable," I say. "But isn't Uber supposed to make it easier and cheaper to hail a cab? You're just one click away from instant door-to-door service. I still don't understand why the taxi-drivers are so upset."

"Oh, so you're one of these high tech gurus, are you?"

"Well, not really," I say defensively.

"Can't get enough of your fancy devices, eh? Look, if you ask me, it's a crying shame when an honorable trade is taken over by eggheads. Do you know the Knowledge goes back to the days of Oliver Cromwell?"

In truth, I didn't come looking for an argument but I have to feel sympathy for the Silicon Valley company as I have spent the last three decades of my life in northern California, teaching at a state university close to San Francisco. I'm convinced that smart technology is the driving force behind innovation and a growing economy. After all, I've witnessed a radical transformation in my years as a teacher, from scratchy blackboards to a brave new world of unlimited information and knowledge. And I've tried to adapt my teaching practice to these new digital realities. At my university, the buzz phrase is "disruptive technology." We're told it's a good thing and, by and large, I go along with this, even though I occasionally shudder at the phrase's Orwellian undertones and pine for the good old days when depth of knowledge in your area of expertise counted for something important.

I gaze again at the picture of Mata Hari on the wall, as if seeking guidance, but I can't seem to decipher her inscrutable smile.

Fortified by more beer, I feel ready to push my thoughts further. "Isn't Uber just putting power into the hands of the customer?" I say. "After all, you're not going to stop progress. The Luddites couldn't prevent machines from taking over the jobs of textile workers."

Again, he burps; this time, it feels purposefully malicious. "You know," he growls, "they say that people with the Knowledge use parts of the brain that the average Joe doesn't even know exists. Are you telling me that you want to see that kind of genius disappear forever?"

My phone rings to a familiar Beatles tune. I check the number. It's an international call, from my wife. I've not spoken to her since arriving in England to attend a five-day conference on multiculturalism at London University. I grab the phone, bury it in my jacket pocket, and make a mental note to call her later.

"Sorry!" I smile sheepishly.

He shakes his head and mutters under his breath.

"By the way, my name is Mark," I introduce myself.

"Pleased to meet you. You can call me Puggy."

"Really?"

"Best not to ask why," he says. "It's a long story."

"Anyway, you were saying about those ghosts?" I realize it's time to move on to another topic.

"Harry and Frances, the ghosts I'm talking about, were convicts. They were kept downstairs beneath us, in a holding cell, while they were waiting to be shipped out to Australia, Botany Bay or some such place. The boat was moored on the river, just a hundred yards or so from here. Well, the day before their departure, they tried to escape but in their haste fell down a sink-shaft and died in each other's arms, so the story goes. You have to realize, all of this happened back in Queen Victoria's time so it's become something of a lost secret by now. But I know they still walk the tunnels. In fact, I can feel their presence at this very moment."

I try hard not to laugh. The story is far-fetched for sure, but at least it's more entertaining than a heated discussion about the perils of disruptive technology.

"You don't believe me, do you?" he asks.

"How do I know you're not pulling a fast one on me?"

"It's all part of the Knowledge, mate. You've either got it or not."

At this point, I'm beginning to feel like I'm part of a practical joke, one with a predictable punch-line. I could go along for the ride and accept the man's banter at face value or I could take things in a completely different direction.

"I tell you what," I say brightly. "I'll show you what modern knowledge looks like. I'm going to ask Siri a few questions about these ghosts."

"Who's Cindy, for heaven's sake?"

"Siri. She's my knowledge navigator. She knows everything."

"She lives inside that little box of yours, does she? You've got to be kidding me, mate. I hope I never see the day when these things take over our lives, let alone try to imitate human beings."

"Don't worry," I laugh. "I know when to draw the line between man and machine."

"God help us all, that's what I say. Go on then! Let's see what your little Frankenstein can do."

"All right, Siri. Here we go. I'm sitting in a pub called The Morpeth Arms, on the west bank of the River Thames. Can you find it?"

"*Yes, Mark,*" she answers dutifully. "*It is located at 58 Millbank, opposite Riverside Walk Gardens, close to Vauxhall Bridge.*"

"Very good, Siri. Now, there is a gentleman sitting beside me who goes by the name of Puggy. He claims there are ghosts under this pub. What do you know about that?"

"*I can tell you that the Morpeth Arms is famous for its spies on account of its location directly opposite the MI6 building. Upstairs, there is a picture of Mata Hari, one of the most famous spies of the twentieth century.*"

"Yes, I am sitting nearby. She looks tantalizing, I must say. But what about the ghosts?"

"*On the issue of ghosts I am not permitted to speculate.*"

"Siri, don't you believe that ghosts exist?"

"There is no definitive answer to your question, Mark."

"Does that mean you don't know?"

"I know what I don't know," she says.

"That sounds like a rhetorical tautology, Siri."

"Thank you for the compliment, Mark. You are most welcome."

Puggy looks up at the ceiling. "What a load of codswallop," he hisses. "Look, mate, I can tell you more about local history than your fancy digital friend. Take the Tate Gallery, for example."

"The Tate? I love that museum. I have fond memories of taking day trips there when I was a kid growing up in Somerset. I used to spend hours in the Turner collection. I was there this morning, as a matter of fact, remembering the good old days. "

"Yes, but do you know what the place used to be?"

"Well, I assume it's always been some kind of national museum. At least, that's what I've been told."

He grins and burps. "A prison for petty thieves and riffraff, that's what it was," he says matter-of-factly. "The prisoners were moved to the tunnels right under this pub and then to the river site just down from here where they would be loaded onto ships and transported to Australia. Hundreds of them. All ghosts now, of course, like Harry and Frances."

"And how do you know this, Puggy?"

"I just do, mate." Then he winks. "Go ahead and ask your friend, Sibyl, or whatever she's called."

"I suppose this is all part of the Knowledge," I say, trying to contain my sarcasm. "OK. I'll ask Siri."

In a jiffy, she responds in her usual pitch-perfect tone: *"The Tate Gallery stands on the site of Millbank prison which was opened in 1816 and closed in 1890. A buttress can be found at the head of the river from which until 1867 prisoners sentenced to transportation embarked on their journey to Australia."*

He looks at me, arms folded, with a broad smile on his face. "Fair enough," I say.

I realize it's time for more drinks. I go to the bar for another round. The bartender pulls the pints and chuckles, "Having a nice chat with the Admiral, are you?"

"Yes, he's quite a character, isn't he? Seems to burp a lot. Why on earth is he called the Admiral? He told me his name was Puggy."

"Ah, well, it's to do with all those stories he likes to tell about sailing the seven seas—Australia, the Far East, the South Pacific, all the far-flung corners of the Empire. He'll bend your bloody ear about his adventures if you let him. Isn't that what he's been doing for the last hour or so with you?"

"No, thank God. But he did tell me about the ghosts downstairs," I say. "What do you know about them?"

He stiffens. "Sorry, sir. We prefer not to talk about that particular subject around here. It's strictly off limits, if you know what I mean."

That's strange, I think to myself. Perhaps Puggy was speaking the truth when he said you have to be careful what you say in this pub. Clearly, there are still some secrets that are too sensitive to disclose—mainly to do with spies, ghosts, or even lunatics, it appears.

"Well, what does the Admiral do for a living?" I ask, changing the subject.

"No one knows. He just comes and goes as he pleases. We don't even know where he lives. He just sits in that corner and babbles away. Usually, people leave him alone and don't touch him with a barge pole. You must have a soft spot." He makes a gesture to his head. "He's a bit of a nutcase," he whispers. "Anyhow, enjoy the drinks and beware of the spies, especially Mata Hari." Then he gives me a wink and a nod.

I pretend to share the joke but, in truth, I'm starting to feel annoyed by the fog of evasion that seems to circulate around here rather like the cigarette smoke that used to fill these pubs in my old student days.

I ferry the drinks back to our table. "The bartender claims you were quite a sailor," I say.

He smirks. "I can tell you stories about the sea and the sky and your friend, Mr. Turner, until you're blue in the face," he says. "Do you have a favorite painting of his?"

"'Sunrise with Sea Monsters,'" I say, perkily. "I've often wondered about the giant fish eye in the lower left corner. You don't see it from a distance. But when you get close to the canvas, all of a sudden—there it is!"

"Ah, that's the beauty and the mystery of it, see? It's subtle. It seems to come out of nowhere." He moves his face closer to mine again, only this time I catch a strong whiff of raw onions on his breath. "There's another secret about that painting," he says. "It was not meant to be about sea monsters at all. That's just the way it came out. It was intended to be a picture of morning mist rising above the English Channel. That's how art happens sometimes. You don't intend it to be a certain way but it assumes its own identity and takes its own course. It's quite magical, eh?"

"Yes, it's a mystery all right," I say, recoiling slightly from the pungent aroma. "Usually, I try to be logical about these matters but for once I'm prepared to believe in what you say."

Predictably, he burps, perhaps out of appreciation. Only this time, he grabs his stomach as if he is in considerable pain.

"Are you OK?" I ask.

"Nothing to worry about," he says with a grimace. "I'll be alright in a jiffy. But it's time for me to head home. I'll leave you in the company of ghosts and spies."

I insist on helping him outside and we totter downstairs, arm in arm, towards the exit.

We leave the pub. The rain has stopped and the sun is shining. The buildings and streets seem miraculously transformed by the brilliant light and I feel some of my bright American optimism returning. Or perhaps it's just the beer talking.

"How are you getting back to your hotel?" he asks.

"I'll walk, I suppose. Besides, it's probably best not to take the Underground, let alone an Uber taxi, now that I have discovered the Knowledge, thanks to you." I afford a chuckle, thinking it's a clever parting gesture to make to my new friend.

"That's the spirit," he says, laughing at my pleasantry. "At least, you've learned some useful knowledge to take back to your home in golden California."

"The usual secrets and lies," I joke.

"Yes, watch out for the ubiquitous electronic eye," he says. "And remember this: the Sun is God." He burps, then walks away.

After a few paces, I stop. I've heard that phrase before but I can't quite put my finger on where exactly. I take out my phone. "Siri, who said 'the Sun is God?'"

On cue, she answers: *"These were the last words spoken by the English landscape painter, J. M. W. Turner."* She continues, *"By the way, Mark. You may be interested to know that Admiral Puggy Booth was a pseudonym used by Mr. Turner to conceal his real identity from prying neighbors."*

"Well, well," I say out loud. "The crafty old bugger. Thanks, Siri. I really don't know what I'd do without you."

I continue to walk towards Whitehall, past a row of conspicuous surveillance cameras mounted on lampposts. I've been in London for less than twenty-four hours but I feel that I've learned one or two new things about the country where I grew up but abandoned as a young man. With a stretch of imagination, perhaps I really was conversing with the spirit of Joseph Turner. No, that's rubbish, I realize, and continue walking.

Just as I turn the corner, another question pops into my mind. "Siri, did Mr. Turner have dyspepsia?"

There's a brief silence. Then she does something I didn't even know she was capable of doing. She burps, without so much as an apology.

Die Into Life

Fran Brown settled down to watch the evening news when the house telephone rang. Her eldest son picked up the receiver and paused before handing the phone over to her. "It's for you, Mum," he said.

"Who is it?" she asked.

He shrugged his shoulders and covered the mouthpiece. "An old friend."

Fran took the telephone handle. "Hello?" she inquired cautiously.

"Oh, Fran. This is Ken Samson. I hope I'm not disturbing you." She was looking through the living room window into the darkness of the garden as if the voice of the speaker might be hiding outside, waiting to step into the light. "How are you?" he asked.

"Fine, thanks, fine," she gushed, knowing how intensely her husband Terry disliked any interruption to the evening television ritual. "Listen, Ken, hold on a minute. I'll switch phones."

She sidled into the kitchen and snatched at the receiver. "Hello, Ken? I'm in the kitchen now." She took a deep breath. "It's quite a surprise to hear from you after such a long time." She closed the door behind her. "How many years has it been?"

"I can't remember, Fran," Ken rasped. There was a brief, uneasy silence. "I'm calling because I've got something important to give to you. Something that belonged to John."

"John?"

As soon as her mouth shaped his name, she felt she was bringing back into existence a lover with whom she shared a brief, intense relationship during her student days at the University of London in the 1970s. She recalled his tall and thin figure, his angular face with pockmarks and scraggly sideburns, and the shaggy brown sweater that he was so fond of wearing. It was as if his image had been hibernating in her subconsciousness for over two decades, ready to impose itself at a moment's notice.

"Can you come up to London tomorrow?" Ken asked. "If you take the morning coach, I can meet you somewhere near the station."

She considered her family. How would they cope without her for the day? Who would pack their lunch boxes? On the other hand, she reasoned, Terry could drive the two boys to school and she could take the day off with sick leave. With a quickness that surprised and excited her, she decided to make the journey.

They agreed to meet the next day at noon in the Half Moon Pub opposite Victoria Coach Station. This would allow her to catch an early morning coach from Somerset to London, meet with Ken, walk around a little, and then be home in time for a late supper. A day's outing like this, she thought, would hardly disturb the evenly-keeled routine of her life.

She put the phone down and looked around the kitchen at the symbols of a twenty-year marriage: pots hanging obediently on their hooks, cheery family snapshots on the refrigerator door, a breakfast table neatly laid out for the morning. How different, she thought, to the time in her life when she lived as a student squatter in an abandoned house in north London, along with John and Ken. But she couldn't afford to develop the thought further, not now at least.

She returned to the living-room where three faces stared passively at the TV screen. "Who was it?" her husband asked indifferently.

"An old friend from university. He says there's a surprise reunion party in London tomorrow. I'd like to go. I could get the day-return coach."

She felt ashamed of her deceit. But telling the whole truth at this time would be too complicated, she thought.

Her husband squeezed her hand and returned his attention to the television. The image of a mangled car in a crowded Jerusalem street filled the screen. Later that night, Fran had a dream in which the image of a bomb blast was superimposed on the screaming face of a blood-soaked victim. She awoke with a shudder as she recalled that the face in her dream was John's.

□□□□□

Sitting on the coach for the three-hour trip to London the next morning, Fran was able to reflect back on her time with John. She was a first-year student at the University of London, fresh from the provinces. He was a trainee at St. Guy's Hospital, more inclined towards poetry and philosophy than to the medical sciences. He called his field of study, "the metaphysics of existence." She remembered how they met at the Roundhouse Theatre in Camden. He was sitting behind her at a production of Kafka's *The Trial*, and said to her at the end of the play, "Excuse me, do you know the quickest way out?"

"Is there a way out?" she had responded with a timid laugh.

"Well," he chuffed. "What do I say to that?"

While she stumbled over an answer, he invited her for a drink. She went along and was attracted by the awkward way he hunched his shoulders over a glass of beer and how skillfully he rolled his cigarettes. That night, on an impulse, she decided to move out of her college dormitory and into John's small flat. A free-floating life of recreational drugs, jazz music, and bohemian literature awaited her, she thought.

"Be your own God," John had insisted. At first, it felt like a liberating and intoxicating mantra to Fran.

But the experiment quickly spiraled out of her control as John's day-long acid trips, or soul adventures as he called them, gradually became insupportable. To save money, they occupied an empty building as a legal squat, joined by Bruce and Sylvia, dropouts from St. Guy's Hospital who were living on unemployment benefits. The squat was organized by Ken, a card-carrying member of the Socialist Worker's Party who was trying to change the world "one comrade at a time."

Now, looking back, Fran wondered if she had experienced anything like true happiness with John. Yet despite her lingering doubts, there had been something about his uncompromising commitment to life which continued to intrigue her. Yes, he was a cruel bully, but he also possessed a manic intensity that both frightened and fascinated her.

She remembered one particular letter he had written after she temporarily abandoned the squat. "I must have you," he wrote. "Perhaps you think of me all day as I do of you? I want you to give up your whole heart to me. Only then will we have the perfect relationship, sealed in eternity." At the time, she didn't know whether to cry or laugh out loud.

□□□□□

She began to notice familiar landmarks out of the coach window: Chiswick overpass, Hammersmith Odeon, Fuller's Brewery, the Thames Embankment. Slowly, the coach worked its way through the traffic of central London and then, as slight drizzle started to fall, it pulled into Victoria Coach Station.

As she stepped down from the coach, she was struck by the thick sootiness of the London air. The noise, the traffic, the diesel fumes, even the soft rain seemed to add to the thickness. In the twenty years that she had been living away from the city, she had forgotten this peculiar sensation but its familiarity came back to her now. She found it strangely exciting.

She spotted The Half Moon Pub on the opposite side of the street, crossed over, and went inside. It was crowded with travelers and office workers on an early lunch break. She sidled through a press of bodies and walked the length of the bar before recognizing Ken in the far corner of the room at a small round table.

"Hello Ken," she said, extending her hand.

Without a formal greeting, he asked, "What will you have?"

She was slightly offended, after all these years, but not entirely surprised given Ken's harshness towards Fran in the past. As she took a seat, she said, "Just a coffee, please. Thanks."

She was struck by Ken's appearance. She remembered him as being trim and fit, but now he appeared thin, gaunt, and exhausted. There was a sizeable tear on the sleeve of his jacket. As he returned with the drinks, she noticed how he labored to keep his balance. Nervously, he placed her coffee on the table.

"You're looking well, Fran," he said.

"Thanks!" she replied. "I can't complain. I have a wonderful family and home, after all."

"A home," he repeated. He looked at his half pint of beer with a mixture of contempt and wistfulness. "Yes, that's more than I ever had or wanted for that matter." He paused. "But, Christ, let's not talk about me."

"Oh, come on, Ken," she teased. "After all this time, surely I'm entitled to a bit of probing. What have you been up to, anyway? I mean, the last time I heard from you was donkey's years ago. I think Bruce and Sylvia told me you were starting a small business."

"Nothing came of it," he said sharply. "It was just a pipedream." There was a short silence before Ken resumed: "Have you been in touch with Bruce and Sylvia, then?" he asked.

"Four or five years ago now, I think. Are they still working in the Village?"

Ken looked away and said: "Yeah, they're doing well. They own a New Age shop in Hampstead. I think it's called Zeno's. They're still into their touchy-feely ways." She noticed some of the old magic in Ken's dancing, intelligent eyes. She remembered how his face used to light up when, on a cold and grey winter's afternoon, he would take the first drag of a cigarette, follow it with a sip of hot tea, then exclaim, "Ah, a lovely cuppa, that is!"

But he seemed more burdened now. He continued: "Remember how weird we thought all that stuff was? Tarot cards, healing stones, Ouija boards? It seems that Father Time has rewarded the lovey-dovey couple, don't you think?"

She shrugged and looked around at the well-to-do customers bantering gaily over their ploughman's lunches. Ken continued his thought: "We each tried our own experiments back in the good old days, didn't we? I suppose nowadays we're simply living out the natural consequences of those experiments, for better or worse." He paused again.

"Except you, Fran. You're the one who changed direction altogether by settling into a nice and quiet life. You look better for it. I mean that!"

"What about John?" she said, returning her attention to Ken. "He was an exception too, surely!"

"Oh no, he lived out the consequences to the fullest," Ken replied without hesitation. "He took the ultimate trip. He died while he was most alive. Young, fit, and intellectually curious. No, he wasn't the exception. He was the truest expression of what we were all about."

"Come off it, Ken," she answered quickly. "He took his own life, for heaven's sake. He betrayed me. He betrayed you. He betrayed himself. Where's the loyalty in that?"

She had wanted to sound resolute but she realized, from Ken's sullen expression, that she might have been over-forceful, perhaps even insensitive to the occasion. A change of subject was needed.

"Anyhow, you never answered my question. What are you up to these days?"

He drained his glass then said, "I suppose you haven't heard. How could you, living so far away all this time?" He looked into her eyes and said, "I'm dying of AIDS. Actually, it's been going on for quite a while. According to the doctor, I've probably got less than six months left. So I get visits from hospice once a week. The nurses have been bloody terrific."

"God, Ken, I'm so sorry."

"That's OK," he said. "Besides, I didn't invite you to London for a weep session. Anyhow, you don't need to worry about me. I may look a bit frail and fragile on the outside but I'm happy inside. I really am. Look! I'll even flash a royal smile for you." He opened his mouth wide like a Cheshire cat but she only noticed the deep crease lines around his cheeks.

"The joke is," he continued. "I've never felt as much alive. Hard to believe it, but I'm enjoying saying my fond farewells to old friends and lovers. It's quite a privilege. Which is more than John ever had."

He reached into his duffel bag and brought out a book and small wooden box which he placed on the table. She recognized the copy of Keats's *Complete Poems* that she had shared with John. Its black vellum cover had faded with age yet lost none of its smoothness. She opened it and saw their signatures in light blue ink: "John and Franny, September 1971, Hampstead." She was tempted to turn the pages but recoiled and hastily put the book down, next to the box.

"And what on earth is this?" she asked, fingering the small wooden container.

"John's gift. He bought it for you a few days before jumping to his death. He meant to give it to you on your birthday. But do you remember how strangely he behaved that week? He seemed totally out of sorts. Besides, I was too jealous to remind him."

"Jealous?" she asked, surprised by the word.

She noticed that his eyes began to redden. "Because I was madly in love with him. And I never told him. I never got the chance to tell him."

There was an uneasy pause. She needed to absorb this new information. True, Fran and John had never fully appreciated Ken's presence in the house. They acknowledged his quiet intelligence but rarely engaged it, preferring instead to deride him for his shyness and social awkwardness. It was as if they had relegated him to the shadowy background of their lives. Why hadn't she been able to see any possible amorous connection between Ken and John? She couldn't begin to imagine John and Ken as would-be-lovers.

"Ken," she said. "I realize I owe you a profound apology. God! I never knew. Honestly, I just …"

"No need, no need," he waved her off.

"No, I insist. Look, I didn't know what the hell I was doing back then. None of us did, really. Quite honestly, I've been happy to put those days behind me. They were too intense, do you know what I mean? After all, we've got to get on with our lives. So I mean it when I say I'm sorry for anything I did to upset you, especially concerning John. You know that, don't you?"

He gave a quiet acknowledgment then said: "Here, open the box. It's a ring. It was intended for your engagement. He was going to surprise you. He wanted to go the whole way. You know, 'till death do us part,' the works."

She opened the box and fingered the ring. It was smooth gold, simple yet elegant.

"This isn't easy for me, Ken. I don't think I can accept this," she said. "Why don't you keep it?"

"Oh, for heaven's sake, this is your ring. It symbolizes what you shared with John. How can you deny that?" He placed the ring into the palm of her hand.

"But it's the symbol of a lie, Ken. Don't you see? The very same week he was going to give me this ring, he took his own life. Is that crazy or what?"

"It's all very well to say that now, twenty years later. But let's face it, Fran, at the time we couldn't see the lie. Maybe it's because we were living too close to the madness."

□□□□□

By the time they left the pub, rain was falling hard. They huddled together under an umbrella and made their way to Victoria underground station. She gently supported him while they took steps down into the station. As they waited on the platform, he said, "I visited the driver of the train a few months after John's suicide."

She took a deep breath as Ken continued: "He was bringing the train into the station and noticed John staggering along the platform. The driver said their eyes met and he saw two circles of fire in John's eyes. Then John went over the edge as if he were jumping into a swimming-pool."

At the time, she had coped with John's death by running away from the thought of it. "Get on with your life, Fran," her father advised. She dropped out of university, moved in with her parents, and resolved to organize her days according to a structured regimen free of drugs and, more importantly, free of John's overpowering personality. Within a year, she had married and settled down in Somerset. Gradually, she released John from her memory, or so she thought.

Ken's train pulled up to the platform. She hugged him and watched him fumble for a seat. "Take care, Ken," she mumbled to herself. She waved as the train slipped away into darkness followed by the furious roar of wind in the tunnel.

As she stood on the platform, alone yet surrounded by passengers rushing in all directions, she felt a sudden trepidation. For the twenty years since John's suicide, she had grown used to an orderly lifestyle surrounded by loved ones. In this way, she had become the mistress of her own fate. Now, here she was without a friend or family member close at hand, with no place to go, in a city that had lost its familiarity to her. Yet she felt strangely alert and alive, ready to follow some unknown and unpredictable path, even if she was uncertain where it might lead.

She took the Northern Line to Hampstead. Forty minutes later, she was walking down Fitzjohn's Avenue, past Zeno's, Bruce and Sylvia's shop. It was hard to miss, with its colorful rocks and soaps, and miniature rock gardens arranged tastefully in the display window. The smell

of incense and the sound of drumbeats poured out of the open door-
way. She scuttled past self-consciously. She thought she saw Bruce's
figure leaning over the counter and, for a moment, she considered dou-
bling back and going inside. But what would she say to Bruce after all
this time? Starting a conversation would require too much effort, she
reasoned. A vague desire urged her to keep moving. So she continued
walking down the street, past clothing boutiques, a bookstore, some
newer restaurants, and a charity shop.

She turned a corner onto Well Walk and suddenly realized that she
had arrived at the old squat where she had lived with John. The abandoned house had been completely refurbished and renovated. There
was even a fence around it now and an alarm system attached to the
outside railings. Two cars were parked in the driveway, yet there were
no obvious signs of human habitation. She stood in front of the house
for a few moments and tried to absorb the changes. This is where I experienced my year of life and death, she marveled. Somewhere in this
house there must surely still exist a memory of those moments with
Ken, with Bruce and Sylvia, with John. Yet how could the new owners
know this? How could they ever feel a similar passion?

Now that she had come this far, she realized she had time for one
last visit to Hampstead Heath before heading back to Victoria Coach
Station.

She skirted the ponds and followed the path up to Parliament Hill.
The sun had disappeared behind the clouds and it looked like more
rain was on its way. The familiar outline of St. Paul's Cathedral and
the British Telecom Tower were visible in the distance. She stopped
to sit on a bench on top of the hill and take in the surroundings.
Everything—the bench, the cluster of oak trees, the shape of the hill-
side, even the sooty dampness of the air—seemed urgently familiar,
yet she knew she had changed so much since she was here last. A particular memory began to replay in her mind with the clarity of a film.

It was the last afternoon they spent together. John had taken a large
dosage of LSD, ninety micrograms. His intention, he said, was to gain
insight into the substance of life—DNA models, the human genetic
structure, and their rearrangement through space and time. While he
was tripping that afternoon, she remained sober. This had become, by

then, the standard arrangement. They had walked onto the Heath making snide comments about the strangers around them. John claimed to see right through the superficiality of them all. She recalled the expression he used that day. "They're out of touch with their inner divinity," he said. The only exception was a solitary kite flyer on Parliament Hill.

"Where is all this going?" he said. "All this movement. People rushing from one place to another." He looked down from the hill at the London lights spreading across a darkening sky. Then he said, "Why can't we live in this moment forever?"

"'And with fierce convulse, die into life,'" she remarked sarcastically, quoting from one of their favorite poems by Keats.

"Well, I'd take that form of existence over being a vegetable," he hissed.

"Or a nutter!" she muttered, more to herself than John.

She hadn't meant to provoke him with her little joke. It's just that she had begun to see his biting cynicism as self-centered and overly indulgent, often at the expense of others. She knew that once the effects of the drug had worn off he would return to relative normalcy and the same dysfunctional routine would go on repeating itself. She didn't anticipate his agitated response to her remark. He flipped up his coat collar and headed hastily down the hill. She didn't know it at the time, but she was watching him walk out of her life, to his death.

On the coach returning home, she wondered if she had been unfairly judging these days of reckless experimentation by the standards she had set for herself in recent years. After all, her family life had settled into an established and predictable routine. Her children performed well in school at sports and academics. Her husband had a secure job as a lecturer in economics at the local college. And she felt grateful to be employed as a systems analyst for a software firm located within walking distance of home. She considered herself a happy and fortunate middle-aged woman, suitably prepared to meet the challenges that might arise in the second half of her life.

These memories of John were rather like the countryside floating by outside the coach, she thought. Out there, the world seemed dark and inhospitable. The outlines of houses and farm buildings appeared like vaguely threatening shapes. Freezing rain continued to clatter against the coach windows. But inside, she felt snug and cozy. John was an adventurer into that dangerous outside world whereas she had developed an appreciation for the comforts and security of a domesticated life. That's why, for the last two decades, she had gravitated towards easygoing, conventional people much like the passengers in the coach around her who were trading chitchat over warm cups of tea and digestive biscuits. She was cheered by their anonymous company.

As the coach pulled into Taunton station, she caught sight of the family car parked next to the bus terminal. The coach came to a halt. She swung her shoulder bag down from the overhead rack and then, on an impulse, reached into her coat pocket for John's engagement ring. But it wasn't there. She turned in panic to her seat.

"My ring! Where is it?" she gasped.

An elderly lady crossed the aisle to help look under the seat. They poked around for several seconds before the coach driver came back to see what the commotion was about. "What's the matter, luv?" he asked.

"She's lost her ring," the lady replied in a sympathetic tone. "It must mean so much to her, the poor dear!" Other passengers were by now turning around to look, some visibly irritated by the holdup.

"What's that on your finger, then, dearie?" the driver said.

Fran raised her left hand to take a look and was astonished at what she saw.

"Oh, I am so sorry. How on earth did that happen?" At some point during the return journey, she realized she must have slipped John's engagement ring onto her middle finger. "I feel like such a fool," she gushed.

"Happens to the best of us," the driver said, patting her on the back. He laughed while other passengers joined in.

Fran stepped down from the coach and was relieved to see her husband and children waiting on the curb, holding hands and beaming at her. As she walked calmly towards them, however, a powerful emotion suddenly welled up inside and she started to sob uncontrollably.

"What's wrong, darling?" her husband asked, kneading her shoulder.

She dabbed her face and smiled weakly. "Oh, nothing really," she said, "It's been such a tiring day with old friends. I'm just happy to be back home where I belong."

The Rally

"I can't stand the lies any longer," David Jones grumbled as he jabbed his thumb at the television screen. "I mean, just look at this man. He's a liar and a hypocrite. You can tell by his eyes. They're shifty."

His wife Clare studied the screen thoughtfully. "Darling, that's the leader of the free world you're talking about," she said.

"The most dangerous in the world, more like," David sputtered. "I don't trust him one bit." He slumped further into his armchair, his shoulders heaving with indignation.

Clare turned sharply to face her husband. "All right, so he's a madman. He wants to start a bloody war. And now he's trying to drag the rest of the world into his evil game. Why don't we do something about it before it's too late, for heaven's sake?"

In the course of her seventeen year marriage, she had become increasingly resigned to her husband's cynical perspective towards authority and the frequent armchair criticism that rarely resulted in practical action. She, on the other hand, maintained a belief in the value of political solidarity. "There's the big rally on Saturday, you know," she continued, brightly. "Everyone's talking about it at work. We could go up to London with the church group. I know they're taking a busload."

He shifted in his chair. "What's the point of going on yet another march?" he said wearily. "The war is going to happen, no matter what. You can see it in the eyes of our so-called leaders. They've already made up their mind."

It was the familiar, repeated excuse for doing nothing. But this time, instead of giving in to defeatism, Clare decided to press her case further. "Well, they'd have a hard time ignoring more than a million demonstrators in the heart of London," she said. "And there will be marches going on all over the world. New York, Rome, Sydney.

Maybe, this is the right thing to do, Dave."

He fixed his attention once again on the television screen, at the shadowy figures behind a podium grinning and shaking hands.

"All right," he said decisively. "Perhaps we should finally teach these bastards a lesson."

His eyes glowed like orbs of fire, she thought.

□□□□□

Demonstrators came from all corners of the land to participate in the rally. Colorful banners proclaimed their diverse allegiances: the Eton George Orwell Society, Oxford Women's Institute, the Cardiff Anarchists, the Bradford Muslim Association. Protesters hoisted placards reading NOT IN MY NAME, DON'T ATTACK IRAQ, and NO WAR FOR OIL.

Clare and David marched with a small group carrying a banner with a picture of a dove next to the words, QUAKERS AGAINST THE WAR. They sang "Give Peace a Chance" as they processed to the rally's final destination, Hyde Park. It was a cool, sunny February afternoon and the winter light was already beginning to fade into oncoming evening.

"Two million plus," roared a steward on his megaphone. "You are now officially part of the largest ever public protest in British history." The marchers cheered as they continued past the upscale shops of Piccadilly, past the Wellington monument, and into Hyde Park.

"How are you feeling, Dave?" Clare asked.

"Better, thanks!" he said.

She hoped the rally might be uplifting for them both, especially for David. Fatigue had overwhelmed him in recent years, punctuated by occasional bursts of optimism. They had tried several therapies to stabilize his moods: counseling, Prozac, meditation, acupuncture, even a course in organic gardening. Yet the stubborn lethargy stuck to David like a morning fog that blocks out the sunshine, refusing to lift.

He seemed more animated now, she thought.

"Look Clare!" He pointed at two oversized puppets of George Bush and Tony Blair locked together in an intimate embrace like Siamese twins. As the puppets trundled down the street in an awkward dance, passersby jeered and mocked them. A carouser outside a pub lifted his pint glass and hailed, "Long live the United States of Great Britain!"

David and Clare shared the joke. It was the kind of antiauthoritarian humor they had enjoyed together through the years.

In Hyde Park, they joined hands with others to listen to keynote speakers. At first, there was the decorated soldier who announced, "I am not against military intervention where it is justified but there is no reason for this at all." Then there was the pop star who asked, "How long will you so-called leaders of the free world lie and deceive our country speaking so many words but so few truths?" Then there was the prize-winning playwright who thundered, "The president of the United States is a bully—a small-minded, petty, backyard bully." Finally, the populist statesman rallied the crowd by leading a chant, "STOP THE WAR! STOP THE KILLING!"

□□□□□

On the way home, inside the heated bus, she nestled her head on his shoulder. "You know what today reminded of," she said softly into his sweater. "The demonstration at Greenham Common when we kicked out the American cruise missiles."

"True," he answered, absently. He stared out of the window, his mind stuck elsewhere.

"I mean it. Today's rally comes from the same passion and positive energy."

He turned to her. "But it didn't make much of a difference, really, did it?"

"Of course it did!" she said, pulling on his sweater sleeve.

"What I mean to say is that the U.S. simply moved their nuclear warheads elsewhere. The rally at Greenham didn't bring an end to their nuclear policy or to that crazy Star Wars scheme of theirs."

"But it was a step in the right direction, Dave," she insisted.

He angled his face more closely to hers. "But, darling, that's not the point, don't you see? The Americans deliberately lost the battle of Greenham Common so that they could win the larger war of nuclear supremacy."

"Oh, come off it. That's going too far."

"Is it?"

They looked around the bus self-consciously, realizing they had raised their voices. Apart from a couple gently bantering in the back seat, all other passengers were dozing. She squeezed his hand and smiled reassuringly. "Anyhow, it was a lovely day," she said. "I'll remember it for a long time."

"Yes," he replied dreamily.

"The leaders can't afford to ignore our message of peace any longer. I mean, it was so loud and clear. The whole world heard it today. It's going to make a difference. Don't you agree, darling?"

He turned away to look through the window, at the gloomy fields and shadowy outline of trees against the night. It was as if he were peering into the complex landscape of his own mind, at some ominous portent of the future that was connected to unsettled ghosts from the past.

"No, I doubt it," he said, with understated conviction. "I don't think it will make much of a difference."

She caught his reflection in the window, the sloping shoulders and the empty eyes, and felt his listless hand slip out of her grip.

Beyond the Pale

Sammy Law was folding a copy of *The Evening Standard* newspaper when a bomb blast slammed him against the wall at the back of the newsagent's shop.

Usually at this time, 5:45 p.m. on a weekday, the shop would fall quiet after the rush of workers had left their Canary Wharf offices and he could nip outside for a quick break. But today, for whatever reason—latest predictions on the evening's football derby between Spurs and the Gunners, breaking news on the Dayton Accord, or rumors of an end to the IRA ceasefire—a sudden rush of customers preoccupied him and his assistant, Ranjit, and this prevented him from taking his routine cup of tea and cigarette. The last customer had just walked out of the shop, and Sammy had started to fold the remaining newspapers into neat piles, when the explosion ripped through the building.

All day long, he had anticipated the night's big football match between local rivals, Arsenal and Tottenham. His excitement peaked with the arrival of his friend, Joe Toft, a few minutes earlier.

"Who's gonna take the cake then, Joey?" Sammy had asked.

"The Gunners, mate!" whooped Joe, waving an invisible banner in the air. "Are-sen-al!" he chanted and leaned over the counter towards Sammy.

Sammy said: "I'm not so sure of the Gunners these days. They should never have gotten rid of the big man, Niall Quinn. Dominant in the air, he was. Get the ball to Niall and he'd bang it home. That's what we're missing, the big fella up front."

Joe shifted his weight menacingly. "What you talking about, you daft bugger? Too slow, ain't he? Liam Brady, he's my man. Nifty as a greyhound. Deadly in the box."

"You're right there, son," said Sammy, happy to find a theme they could agree on.

"But, still, he's not a true Gunner, is he? Not like Merson. Now there's a local boy who came up through the ranks, see? He made it to the top the hard way, polishing the boots of other players. Look at him now! He's playing for England with three lions on his shirt."

"A bit like you, then, Sammy, is he?" Joe gently scoffed. "Making it to the top. Is that where you're headed with this rock band of yours?"

"Knock it off, Joe. No need to get sarky."

Joe elbowed Sammy. "Just pulling your leg, you old geezer." He turned and glanced out the shop window. "Looks like there'll be some bovver on the terraces tonight between the boot boys. You heard anything about that, eh?"

Sammy said: "Yeah, the word is there'll be trouble. Things look as if they might go off at any moment." He followed Joe's gaze as they watched a police car speed past outside.

Joe turned and looked Sammy in the eye. "Is that so? Well, I'm here to say: you stay out of it this time around, Mister Law, all right?" There was mock self-righteousness in his voice.

"Come off it, Joe. You know as well as me, those days are past, mate!" Sammy replied in earnest. "I'm as good as gold now." He smiled uneasily. "Still, if a Spurs supporter gets me going, I'd stick it to him, no question. There's no messing with me. Just ask Ranjit here."

They both turned their attention to Ranjit who was sitting behind the counter, listening closely to the conversation. Aware that some kind of response was expected of him, he answered softly, "Yes, that's right."

"Gives you a hard time, does he, Ranjit?" Joe asked affably, and edged closer towards him.

"Sammy's not too bad. Can't complain!" Ranjit replied with a forced smile.

"Yeah, well, I wouldn't get on his bad side, that's all I'll say. I've seen him when he's had one too many drinks and it's not a pretty picture, believe me. Like when I saw him down at the Half Moon Pub last Saturday night. Screaming blue murder, he was!" Turning to Sammy, he continued: "What's with you and your girlfriend, anyway? You both seemed to be in a right tizzy that night."

"You never saw nothing, you fibber. We were having a nice smooch, that's all."

"Come off it, mate, that's not what she told me. She said, how come Sammy sings the most beautiful ballads on stage, but in real life he's a right bastard?"

Ranjit chuckled while Sammy looked uncomfortable. "She never said that! You lying sod! Don't believe a word of it, Ranjit. He's egging me on, you see. He wants a bit of bovver."

Sammy crouched into a boxing pose and threw a couple of shadow punches at Joe who stealthily side stepped out of the way and laughed.

"If only it were that easy, mate! Some juicy punches on the terraces and a few pints down at the local with the boys. But it's not as simple as that, is it, Sammy? Let's face it, son, your life's a bloody mess!"

There was an uneasy silence. Then Joe studied Ranjit for a few moments as if he were looking for an opportunity to change his line of attack.

"Where are you from, Ranjit, if you don't mind me asking?"

"Lay off him, Joe," said Sammy. "He's one of us, ain't you, Ranjit? Born and bred a true Brit!"

Ranjit trained his eyes on a distant wall. "My dad's from Punjab. I was born in Bromley."

"Are you one of them sicks, then?" There was a friendly menace in Joe's voice. "How come you don't wear a funny bandage around your head, eh?"

"We're not Sikhs. We're Hindu."

"Whoops, sorry mate," Joe chuckled. "I'm getting into deep shit here, I can tell. Ethnic cleansing and all that. I'd better stay clear of that particular minefield. Still, who are we to talk?" He turned away to look at Sammy. "Just look at us and the Irish. Been at each other's throats for hundreds of years. Can't understand it, myself. I reckon this latest cease-fire has just about had it. It's going to go off again sooner or later."

"Yeah, typical, ain't it?" Sammy pitched in, relieved once more that they had struck a common chord. "More violence on the way. That's all these bloody hoodlums can think about. And who is that suffers every time? Innocent bystanders who've got nothing to do with the problem to begin with, that's who."

Joe warmed to the theme. "I ask you, when's it going to stop? After so much blood has flowed under the bridge, when's it going to stop, eh?" He paused. "And on that positive note, I shall leave you two buggers in peace. See you at the game later, Sammy."

"All right. Ta ta, mate."

Joe snatched his newspaper, tucked it under his arm, and walked out of the shop. The tinkle of the doorbell was followed, moments later, by the crash of a 1,000 pound bomb.

□□□□□□

The night air was soon thick with sirens. There was shock and panic on the street. To Charlie Riley, poetry came to mind: "All changed, changed utterly, a terrible beauty is born." The previous six hours had left him feeling nervously exhausted. So much could have gone wrong. Had Frank set the fuse-timer correctly? Had the unit commanding officer called in the coded messages? Had the police emptied the building in time?

The operation had been as clear and logical as a mathematical equation when his cell had planned it. There was beauty also in its execution: taking delivery of the lorry, driving it along the prearranged route through the East End, parking it in the underground car park by the Wharf building. It was all so beautiful, he half expected the arm of God to reach down from the sky and scoop him up either out of anger or approbation, he wasn't sure which.

Eighteen months earlier, Charlie had volunteered as an Irish Republican Army activist after his eldest brother had been fatally shot by an Ulster constabulary patrol in Portadown. Charlie immediately took his place as an active cell member. It seemed the right thing to do. At first, his duties consisted of going door-to-door on the Poleglass estate of Belfast selling "The Republican News." Then, one rainy winter evening, Charlie had been summoned by a top brass of the Army Council to a small, smoke-filled office on the Falls Road in west Belfast.

"Are you ready to play the patriot game, Charlie?" a man, dressed in brown corduroys and bright polo-neck sweater, had asked in a calm voice. He was sitting behind a large desk cluttered with photographs of Gaelic football teams.

"What have you got in mind?" Charlie replied. He heard whispers coming from the hallway beyond the room.

"I'll spell it out for you." The man in corduroys chose his words deliberately. "We want someone with a clean book to pull off a major spectacular on the mainland." He puffed lightly on a cigarette. "And we think you're the one."

Charlie shot a glance through the window at the grey buildings outside then returned his attention to the man and said matter-of-factly: "I'm interested."

"Good lad! We're going to hit hard this time. The whole peace process is going off, you know?" Charlie nodded and studied the man's thick-rimmed glasses. "But before we go any further, Charlie, I must be absolutely certain that you're ready for this." There was softness in the man's voice. "Are you prepared to be a martyr for the cause? Are you prepared for what it takes, Charlie lad?"

Charlie took the cigarette that was offered to him. He already knew the answer to the questions, but wanted to savor the moment. He sucked on the cigarette and inhaled deeply. "What happens later? After the spectacular?"

"You scarper."

"Where?"

"No guarantees, Charlie. I'll be perfectly honest with you. Here are the scenarios. Number one: you muck it up and blow yourself to smithereens which is not advisable. Number two: you get caught which is automatic jail for life. In the Maze if you're lucky, but it's more likely to be the Scrubs. Number three: you get home safe and sound and we'll take of care of you, no questions asked." He paused. "There's one more possibility."

"What's that?"

"We send you Stateside. You'd have a new name and identity. It'd be a new life. Not everyone's cup of tea, mind you."

Charlie stubbed out his cigarette with precision. He had rarely felt so clearheaded. "All right, then. We're on!"

The man looked at Charlie, coolly and impassively, before saying, "Good luck, lad. Now take this and bugger off." He handed over a tricolor flag. Charlie wasn't sure whether it was intended as a good-luck charm or a drape for his own coffin.

Three weeks later, Charlie slipped across the Irish Sea, arriving in London on Christmas Day. He settled into his digs and made contact with Sean and Frank, the other members of his unit. Apart from treating themselves to a New Year's drink at a local pub, they kept a low profile.

Once the date was set for the major spectacular, plans quickly materialized. The lorry, packed with Semtex, would be collected at lunchtime by Sean. Frank would set the fuse timer to go off during the early evening rush hour. Later in the afternoon, Charlie would drive the lorry to the ground level parking lot adjacent to the Canary Wharf building.

Apart from stalling the lorry at a zebra crossing, Charlie executed his part of the mission with clinical efficiency.

Now, in the aftermath of the explosion, as he retreated further away from Canary Wharf, he could begin to envision some kind of future for himself. He felt light-headed and elated. Once clear of London, he would petition the Army Council to send him to the States. It would mean abandoning his homeland, he knew, but that was part of the terrible beauty being born. Again, poetry came to mind: "Out-worn heart, in a time out-worn, Come clear of the nets of wrong and right." It was time to come clear of the nets altogether, he realized. The major events of his life had anticipated this moment of release and liberation.

□□□□□

Six weeks earlier, the paths of Sammy Law and Charlie Riley had crossed inside a pub in north London.

Sammy was playing with his band, The Rockabillies, at a New Year's party in the game room of The White Horse Inn. The night had gone well. A mixed crowd of young and old was enjoying Sammy's repertoire of western swing, country, and soft rock ballads.

Charlie, Frank, and Sean were at the pub for their only binge while on the mainland. Politics was strictly off-limits. Charlie and Sean wore dark sweaters and blue jeans; Frank was in a navy-blue blazer and black trousers. An open packet of Woodbine cigarettes lay on the table.

Frank ferried a round of drinks past the makeshift stage and over to the table. "Nice this, ain't it?" he said as he sat down.

"Can't complain," said Sean.

"Not the same as home, though," added Charlie.

"Ah yes, home." Sean took a long drag from his cigarette. "Hearth, blazing fire, and a tall pint of Guinness."

"Snap out of it, fellas," Frank chimed in. "Don't make me choke!" He smiled and lifted his pint glass. "Let's drink to the future, whatever it might hold for us. Cheers, lads!" They clinked glasses and drank deeply. Frank continued: "So what does the future hold for you, Charlie boy, after this business is over, eh?"

"I'm going to get married to my girlfriend, Rosie. Then we'll go Stateside. I'd like to see the big country, you know, and expand my horizons. Become a new person, like."

"Don't be daft, mate," said Sean, tapping his cigarette on the ashtray. "You'll always be the same person deep down inside. No way you ever gonna change."

"Yeah, dream on, Charlie," Frank said. "The stench of this prison is too strong. It'll always stick to your nostrils. Too much blood has flowed under the bridge, if you ask me. How can you ever turn your back on that strip of land beyond the pale?"

"Fair enough, lads," Charlie said, with a faint smile. "You may call me a bloody dreamer." He looked over at the band. "Anyhow, let's not talk business. Keep it clean, if you don't mind." He emptied his glass. "Drink up. My round, I fancy."

Sean and Frank drained their glasses. "Same again, then, Charlie," said Frank. "Cheers, mate."

Charlie picked up the glasses, headed over to the bar, and placed his order. Sammy, meanwhile, had started a new song whose words Charlie recognized.

"How can I, that girl standing there/ My attention fix/ On Roman or on Russian/ Or on Spanish politics?"

Charlie had memorized the poem as a schoolboy. Hearing the words sung now as a ballad, with a spare piano accompaniment, made an impression on him.

He took the full glasses back to his table, saying excitedly as he sat down, "Beautiful, that! Do you know who wrote the lyrics to that song? It's Yeats, Ireland's poet laureate."

"There he goes again, off into cuckoo land," muttered Frank into the froth of his beer.

Charlie sat and listened raptly as the piano player's solo led gracefully into the concluding verse: "And there's a politician/ That has read and thought/ And maybe what they say is true/ Of war and war's alarms."

Above the general ripple of applause, Charlie clapped his hands vigorously. He raised his glass in the direction of the stage and shouted, "Nice one, lads!"

Sammy responded, "Thank you, ladies and gentlemen. Me and the band will take a quick break for fifteen minutes and then we'll be back for our final set. Hope you can stand the wait."

"Come on, drink up," said Frank. "Let's toast the New Year."

"May it be a good one," said Sean.

"Cheers mates," said Charlie. "Here's to it, then."

"Yeah, here's to you and your beloved Yeats, Charlie boy," said Frank. They clinked glasses.

Charlie stood up. "I'll be right back, lads. Need to take a leak."

He stepped outside and walked over to the men's toilet. Inside, he was greeted by the briny smell of sweat and urine which, combined with the beer he had consumed, made him giddy with nauseous excitement for the New Year.

Sammy was relieving himself into a toilet bowl.

"All right, mate?" Charlie asked as he unbuttoned his fly and moved in next to Sammy. "Yeah, not so bad," said Sammy.

"I enjoyed your set. Especially that last song, 'Politics.'"

"You know it, then, do you?" Sammy looked sideways at Charlie.

"Oh, yeah, I'm fond of Yeats, you might say. But you left off the last couple of lines, you know."

"How does it go, then?" asked Sammy as he tugged at his zipper.

"It's a love song, see, so the poet says at the end, "O that I were young again/ And held her in my arms.' Because all he wants to do, really, is forget the bloody politics around him and love his woman the best way he can."

Sammy nodded in mock appreciation. "All right, mate. I'll keep that in mind for next time." He moved to the door. "Thanks for the tip-off."

Charlie nodded and began to follow. "Are you planning on a tour, then?" he asked.

"The States," Sammy replied. "That's my dream. Graceland, Vegas, LA."

"I hear you. Best of luck."

"Yeah, same to you. And happy New Year!" "Cheers, mate!"

"Ta-ta."

As they stumbled outside, they felt the hopes of the New Year in their bellies. Both were intoxicated by faraway and distant dreams, yet remained unaware how a future convergence would utterly change their tangled destinies.

Why I Wrote *The Jihadi Cell*

In an ideal world, an author should not have to explain, let alone justify, his work of fiction to the reading public. However, because of the growing controversy caused by my recent novel, *The Jihadi Cell,* I feel it's necessary to give some background as to how the story came to be written and why I have grown deeply disturbed by its reception.

The idea for the novel occurred while I was being interviewed by a columnist, Helen Bright, from one of the London weeklies. We were sitting in the lounge of a pub around the corner from the British Museum. It was before the lunchtime rush, and the only other customer was a middle-aged man sitting at the bar chatting with the bartender. She was on assignment to discuss my prize-winning book, *The Ghosts of Stephen Lawrence,* based on the racially motivated murder of Stephen by a gang of white youths in south London on the night of April 22, 1993. The novel took the point of view of the perpetrators and explored the fundamental question: How is it possible to reclaim your humanity after you have committed acts of barbaric violence?

The interview started well enough. She asked about my parents. I told her they moved from Barbados as part of the first wave of Caribbean immigrants to settle in postwar Britain. "Dad worked for London Transport," I explained. "Mum stayed at home and raised two kids. They still live in the same council flat in Camden to this day. It's a small, cramped two-bedroom affair."

Helen nodded her head sympathetically. She had a pleasant, honest face with lively eyes and short, dark hair.

"Don't get me wrong," I continued. "We weren't miserable by any means. My parents were committed to making a go of it in this new land or 'Murda Inglan,' as Mum called it. They were especially keen to pass on to their children a belief in a hard work ethic and self-improvement. In fact, I actually look back on those days with some nostalgia.

I think my parents established a structure and predictable routine to their lives so as to block out the chaos of our surroundings."

"What was your experience of racism while you were growing up?" Helen Bright asked.

The immediacy of her question took me by surprise. I felt she was closing in on something vulnerable and I wasn't sure how to respond at first. Was it the tone of patronizing superiority behind the questions Helen was asking? Or her inviting yet distant smile? I wasn't sure whether I was reading affection or disdain in those light blue eyes.

She seemed to catch my hesitation and quickly added, "Let me go further with the question. How would you describe the current state of race relations several years after the murder of Stephen Lawrence?"

I'm not sure why but instead of answering her directly, I gave an evasive answer, focusing on a troubled relationship I'd had at university. Susie Downing and I lived together for three months in a small flat in Tankerton on the Kent coast, I explained. "It sounds corny, I know. But those were good days for me, full of passion and possibility. We threw ourselves into the hot-button issues of the day—Thatcher, the miners' strike, South African apartheid. Then, it all changed after we visited her family in Yeovil for a long weekend."

"The dreaded encounter with parents from hell, perhaps?"

"Yes, you might say that. Even though Susie claimed she would never allow her parents to dictate her life, it became clear that she intended to heed their advice to 'play safe' and not get caught up in an affair that 'was more trouble than it's worth.'"

I swilled some beer, and then said, "I never loved another with such intensity or tenderness. We were really good for one another." I paused. "Anyhow, so after we split up, I felt emotionally wounded. You ask how I feel about race relations in the wake of the Stephen Lawrence murder case. Well, there's your answer, from the heart."

Helen Bright lit a cigarette, took a puff, and blew smoke out from the side of her mouth, then coolly asked, "So where does your anger come from, Carl?"

I turned my head away, partly out of disdain and partly to buy time for an answer. That's when I set eyes on a curious picture hanging on a nearby wall next to a set of mock Hogarth prints. The picture depicted a large group of blacks in a cozy-looking pub, possibly the same pub we were sitting in at that moment. They were making music with violins and French horns, and dancing with joyous abandon. It was entitled "The Cell," dated 1764. The painter's name, printed boldly at the bottom of the picture, was John Barber.

What immediately struck me about the picture was its portrayal of black men and women amusing themselves, seemingly free of constraints and obligations. And they were doing so several decades before the abolition of slavery in the United Kingdom.

What were they celebrating? And why were they doing so in this bastion of white English culture, the pub? The questions immediately intrigued me, and were a welcome distraction from Helen Bright's intrusive inquiry into the source of my anger.

"I think you're mistaken," I calmly replied after a few seconds. "It's not anger that you see in me. It's pure passion. Sometimes I feel so much love that I have trouble knowing how to express it properly."

Helen stubbed her cigarette into the ashtray and smiled. "Ah, so you are a romantic, after all."

"Of course I am," I bristled. "What other way is there?" All of a sudden, I felt I had been cornered. According to Helen Bright, I was either the angry voice of black Britain or the multicultural ambassador of cool Britannia.

I confess I never read the piece she wrote about me for her magazine. Maybe I was too proud or perhaps I was too afraid. But I did take something valuable from the interview; it was an idea and an experience that I wanted to probe further and shape into a fiction set in contemporary times. This was to become *The Jihadi Cell*.

The novel centered on a circle of friends, second and third generation Caribbean and Middle Eastern Brits who gathered together for bingo and dance nights at a local pub on Camden High Street. Over time, a small number grew disaffected by their dissolute lifestyle as they became increasingly radicalized by the West's endless war on terror and a perceived culture of institutionalized racism.

Leon Trotsky once said, "Those who control the instruments of terror control human emotions." The hard-liners took his message to heart incorporating into their worldview a potent mix of jah love

and jihadi hate. And they didn't have to look far on the internet to receive endorsements and encouragement from any number of fanatical
groups around the world.

At the heart of the novel, the cell orchestrated a series of "spectaculars," the most violent being an explosion that shattered a Trooping
of the Colour parade along the Mall. That act alone claimed the lives
of fifteen bystanders, mostly foreign tourists, and wounded dozens of
others. For several months, members of the cell acted with ruthless
terror, devoting their lives to the pursuit of a single-minded goal: "liberation of the land from the tyranny of a racist, neo-colonialist mindset
and the establishment of a pure caliphate." Britain, they claimed, was
a Dar al-Harb, a land of war, and soldiers who fought valiantly for the
cause would receive an everlasting reward in the afterlife. They would
not give up their killing agenda until the flag of Black Islam could be
seen flying over Buckingham Palace. By the end of the novel, only one
of the cell's ringleaders, Derek Reed, had survived arrest or a bloody
death.

Critics faulted me for taking the point of view of heartless terrorists in telling the story. One tabloid journalist wrote, "Why would the
average reader wish to spend time inside the mind of deranged psy-
chopaths who are the enemies of reason and tolerance?" Yet, I wanted
to demonstrate that so-called terrorists are not born with a terrorist
gene. Derek Reed was a shy and well-educated character. He was born
in 1968 to a middle-class Birmingham family, the son of a successful construction company magnate. A week before his birth, Enoch
Powell had delivered his "Rivers of Blood" speech, outlining the dire
consequences facing Britain in the event of continued mass immigra-
tion from the Commonwealth. Predictably, the speech stirred up anger and anxiety, particularly in the British Caribbean community. My
protagonist was raised in an atmosphere of fear and thick resentment.

I wanted to understand what it was like for Derek Reed to grow
up surrounded by these kinds of toxic emotions, especially as he was
further provoked by the heavy-handed discipline of his paternalistic
father. At the same time, I tried to show that, despite his psychological
wounds and vulnerability, Derek Reed was still capable of love, frac-
tured as it might have been. He experienced a brief yet intense rela-

tionship with Sara, a fellow student at a red-brick university. Together, they enjoyed socializing in the popular hangouts of their college town. But the relationship ended acrimoniously when she realized the extent to which he was trying to control her. "The only person you truly love is the shadow of yourself," she told him finally.

How did his love for Sara metamorphose into an outright rejection of the modern, quotidian life? What transformed a student of civil engineering into a proponent of jihadi terrorism? What fed his explosive hatred of so-called unbelievers and Western civilization? I had hoped that questions such as these might help to stimulate a nuanced conversation about the perplexing and pervasive nature of terrorism in the contemporary world.

Obviously, I neither agree nor sympathize with the motives of a terrorist. But if some critics are unable to distinguish the mind and motives of the novel's protagonist from my own, then I suggest it betrays a failing on their part rather than on mine. Perhaps it is a sign of the uncertain times we live in. When society is driven by feelings of fear and insecurity that are constantly fueled by the inflammatory remarks of political leaders and the unbridled comments of self-righteous bloggers, it's not surprising that I'm suddenly branded as an enemy of the nation. These days, I'm no longer categorized as a British author. Instead, I've been described as a British-based Caribbean author, as if my connection to the land was always based on a temporary rental agreement rather than ownership. Sometimes, I envy my sister Joan, who lives a quiet, orderly life on the same council estate where we grew up, just a few doors away from my parents. "Play it safe, Carl," she insists. "Do yourself a favor."

Yet I do not regret having written *The Jihadi Cell*. And I have not lost my steadfast belief in the importance of understanding—rather than rejecting—the messy contradictions that underpin an inclusive multicultural society. However, I can testify to the fact that it is increasingly difficult to maintain this belief in the violently partisan world we have made for ourselves today.

(Un)done

I.

In the deep bowels of the London Underground, a man steps onto an eastbound train that will carry him from Victoria Station to Upminster. He squeezes into a seat, experiencing the usual press of bodies.

The train hurtles through tunnels, dropping passengers at stations along the way.

Eventually, he finds himself alone except for a woman sitting directly opposite. He is aware of her exotic beauty but does not attempt to make eye contact. Instead, he practices evasive maneuvers that allow for furtive, darting glances. He rubs his chin, kneads his cheeks, and peeks through interlaced fingers.

But her face is turned away.

He crosses his legs, heaves a sigh, and snatches another glance. Her eyes are closed but her mouth is partially and tantalizingly open. He pretends to study an advertisement for women's underwear directly above her head.

He has imagined situations like this before. He has read about them in novels, short stories, and blank verse. He is schooled in the art of fantasy, therefore is not surprised at how easily a poem materializes in his mind:

Come, Lady, come! Reveal to me your worth.
Unzip that velvet dress
Unhook that spangled brassiere
Off with that gold neck-band
Off with those platform shoes
Slip through the G-string

And stand here before me, naked,
Blush-free and beauteous.
License my roving hands, and let them go
Before, behind, between, above, below.
O my Asia, my exotic land
My former colony, my empire, blissfully manned.
How blessed am I in this rediscovering thee
To enter into these bonds is to be free!
My heart quickens, my blood boils.
Your beauty dazzles in the dim light
Of the east-bound train.
Now, as we approach the final stop
At the end of the line,
Pull out your stops
And let me taste the sweet pleasures
Of your forbidden fruit
Until I am, in deed
Done and undone.

II.

The woman has been here before. Not just to this mid-morning train taking her home. Not just to this particular seat in the middle of the carriage, in the middle of the train. But to this situation: the object of another's gaze. She is aware that the man looks at her. Not rudely; not brazenly; not even invasively. But he is looking at her in that most common of ways.

She knows what to do. She has choices. She can play the game. She can close her eyes. She can open her legs provocatively. She can invite his gaze and his intervention. Or she can return his stare and answer him back. She can invade his space, pierce *his* armor of self-confidence. Not with an invitation for sexual communion. But with a defiant challenge: "Who do you think you are, eh? You sodding wanker!"

She knows who she is. She knows her place. She knows herself as an Asian Brit. Exoticized, romanticized, compromised, sexualized. Radicalized and intellectualized.

And with this certainty, with this self-knowledge and self-aware-
ness, she stands up and boldly takes one step towards him:

Yes, I will unfasten my dress
And set my hair free.
I will tease open my body
For your consumption.
Quietly,
I will smooth your skin into peace
My master, my child. Let me teach you
About your hips, your thighs,
Your cheeks, the bones
Of your desire.
Let me revitalize you
Warm this drizzle-dampened soul.
Let me knead your spirits.
But be warned!
I am not used by men, nor do I use them
Rather, I lose them
In the rough seas of my imagination
Where, aroused and afraid,
They give in to my domination
Before they disappear.

III.

The train arrives at the end of the line.

The man and woman exit their carriage, joining a handful of others
who shuffle down the platform towards the Way Out. He follows her
at a measured distance of several yards, unsure whether he is playing
the part of privileged paramour or salacious stalker. At the ticket barrier she wheels left and takes the steps to Upminster High Street. He
follows, then hesitates for a moment. "Do I dare?" he wonders.

While he pauses, a rush of passengers from the Northern line surges
towards him. He struggles against the crowd but is swept back reluc-
tantly to the platform and then through the open doors of a westbound

train. Once again, he finds himself squeezed into a seat between the usual press of bodies, hurtling through tunnels, returning inevitably to Victoria Station, his point of origin.

PART TWO: THEN

□□□□□

The Curious Case
of Miss Irene Adler

To Sherlock Holmes she is always <u>the</u> woman
[Sir Arthur Conan Doyle]

It will come as no surprise to admirers of Sherlock Holmes that the mysteries of the fairer sex were a source of everlasting torment for the great man. While his powers of deduction were legendary, the same could not be said, alas, for his powers of seduction. It was a matter of professional pride, of course, that affairs of the heart were rarely allowed to interfere with his professional work. However, in my ongoing attempt to afford a full and fair account of the life of the world's most famous detective, I feel obliged at this time to speak again of Miss Irene Adler and the curious influence she extended over Holmes long after he had abandoned his Baker Street quarters for his well-earned retirement deep in the Sussex countryside.

The story begins with a most unusual request I received from Holmes that I should make haste to visit him at his home on the Sussex Downs. Naturally, I seized the opportunity to be reunited with my trusted friend after a separation of four years. Indeed, it gave me great pleasure to be seated opposite him again just like in the old days. He seemed to be in jolly spirits, buoyed no doubt by the accoutrements and comforts of his country home. Minutes earlier, the housekeeper had shown me into the living room where he stood, framed at the far end of the room by a large bay window.

"Ah, Watson," he declared in a matter-of-fact manner as if we had been apart for but a day. "How good of you to come!" As he beckoned me to a chair, I found myself uncharacteristically at a sudden loss for words, such was my profound joy.

But I promptly gathered my senses and, after a brief pause, remarked: "Well, Holmes, it appears that bee-keeping and retirement agree with you, eh?" Various books on the science of apiculture were displayed on the table before me, leading me to consider that a jocular comment about my friend's newfound passion in life would not be out of line and might, indeed, serve as the appropriate icebreaker. Finally, I could restrain my admiration no longer. "I say, old chap," I gushed. "I don't think I've seen you looking so robust in quite a while!"

Needless to say, it was heartbreaking for those of us who admired, even loved, Sherlock Holmes to have witnessed his sharp decline in health since solving the case of Mr. Godfrey Staunton in 1898. His spiral into excessive cocaine use, and the increasingly long bouts of idleness and solitude that resulted, have been well documented elsewhere and need not concern us here. As a close confidante of his, I had tried tirelessly to goad him away from his dark habits and was grateful when, at my insistence, he eventually agreed to take a short sabbatical away from the frenetic pace of life at 221 B Baker Street.

I was even more relieved to hear that his initial three-week stay on the Sussex coast had been stretched into a year, then longer, as he settled into the life of a retired gentleman of considerable means. Throughout his protracted absence from London, I kept him close in my thoughts, happy in the knowledge that he was now pouring his tremendous creative energies into the mysteries of bee-keeping. His days of despair were a thing of the past, or so I had imagined.

And so when I received a telegram requesting that I visit him at his Newhaven home, I immediately canceled the day's appointments at my medical practice in the city and booked a day-return ticket on the Paddington to Newhaven train. Besides, the prospect of taking a pleasant excursion through the loamy hills of the South Downs in order to be reunited with my faithful companion was simply too irresistible to refuse.

I was immediately struck by his transformed appearance. He seemed effervescent and robust. His hair was well-groomed and his face lightly bronzed. Perhaps, even more significantly, his thinly compressed lips seemed to have rediscovered the art of shaping themselves into a faintly sardonic smile, and a mischievous twinkle had returned to his eyes.

Indeed, it felt like the good, old days once again as we sat together in the living room. The sun was pouring through the bay window, affording an impressive view of a terraced lawn on which stood rows of white wooden beehives. One could see the light-blue waters of the English Channel in the distance. Infused by a deep sense of well-being, I turned towards Holmes.

"Yes, it is splendid to see you once again, Holmes. Absolutely splendid, I have to confess."

"My dear Watson, it is entirely my pleasure, I assure you." He sat back, crossed his legs, and looked at me intently. Whereas a few years ago his hands might have fiddled nervously with an old black pipe, they now rested comfortably on his lap. He continued, "I notice that married life suits you admirably and that you honor your new wife with considerable devotion."

I blushed slightly. "How so, Holmes?"

He paused before resuming: "It is plain to see that you have gained a pound or two around the midriff. Your cheeks are fuller than when I last see you four years ago, and your moustache is clipped in the Venetian style which, as I gather from my regular reading of *The Times* is the current fashion in London circles. I notice also that you are wearing a continental version of the Oxford shoe. Clearly, you are in the business of impressing someone very dear to your heart and I cannot be so immodest as to believe that person would be me!"

I chuckled, mainly out of embarrassment. "Well really, Holmes! Your feats of deduction and observation are, as usual, most impressive. I cannot hide the fact that Mrs. Watson and I continue to enjoy a felicitous relationship. It appears that you have seen right through me, and not for the first time."

"Capital! This brings me to the business at hand, Watson. Surely, you did not think that I summoned you here for entirely sentimental purposes?"

I leaned closer to him. "Go on, Holmes."

He sprang out of his chair and started to pace the room with hands cupped behind his back. "You say that I have not looked quite as healthy in a long time. On one level, you may be correct, Watson. But now take another look. This time, instead of seeing merely the surface appearance, observe closer if you can."

He leaned over and peered earnestly into my face, almost too boldly if I am to speak the truth.

He continued, "Observe what lies behind these eyes in the recesses of my mind. What do you see now, eh?"

"Why, I sense that you are sorely vexed by something, my dear fellow. Yet I cannot quite fathom what it might be."

He slapped his legs and stepped back with the sprightliness of a prize athlete. "I am indeed troubled, Watson! Beneath this calm exterior, I am truly vexed. And that is why I have called on your services. After all, you are the only person alive who has been granted access to the private life of Sherlock Holmes Esquire!"

"Yes, my good friend, but what is it that ails you so?"

He reached into the breast pocket of his jacket and produced a hastily torn-off newspaper clipping and handed it to me. "Read it!" he beckoned.

I noticed that it had been taken from the previous week's edition of *The Times* and appeared to be an obituary. I started to read: "'Announcement of the death of Irene Adler.'"

I looked up, unable to suppress a slight gasp. "Good heavens! That woman, again!" The mention of Miss Adler's name seemed to have an immediate effect on my eminent friend's countenance. He stood before me, his eyes closed for the moment and his head slightly bowed. Then he said in a soft voice, almost a whisper: "Precisely, Watson. Now read on, please."

I continued reading from the clipping: "'Services to be held at Ramsgate Parish Church on March 15 at 3 p.m.'" I paused. "Why, that was five days ago!"

"Yes, I am aware of that fact, Watson. I have not lost track of time in my dotage, thankfully."

"Well, shouldn't we let sleeping dogs lie, Holmes? No offence intended, of course. But, look here, she *did* cause you considerable embarrassment, you know. And she was the only woman to outwit you during your distinguished tenure at Baker Street." I felt uncomfortable in having to revisit these recollections from the past, fearing that they might trigger a relapse of some sort in Holmes's recent recovery. Yet I recognized, at the same time, a need to offer my moral support. I continued: "It really is a shame that she died so young at the age of, well, let me see, forty-five according to the obituary."

Holmes began to pace the floor once more. "Unfortunately, I cannot let the matter go," he remarked. "My powers of reasoning, in this instance, are not capable of overcoming my natural emotions. I have, over the last ten years, spent considerable time thinking about that woman, and I have to confess that my interests in her have not always been, how shall I put it, professional."

"Now steady on, old chap. There's no need to proceed further if you'd prefer."

"But I do prefer, Watson. In fact, I want you to know that since she bequeathed me this photograph, I have worn it quite close to my heart."

He waved a crumpled wallet-sized photograph before my eyes. I recognized it as the picture of Irene Adler in evening gown that had been given to him during *The Case of the Bohemian Scandal*. I had remarked at the time that she was a lovely woman blessed with a beauty capable of enmeshing any man in the grip of lovesickness. I sensed now that Holmes himself may have succumbed to this malady and had not been entirely successful in shaking off its symptoms.

Holmes continued: "I fear that the announcement of her death, far from putting closure to an unfinished story, has merely reopened the book. Perhaps, indeed, one last chapter has yet to be written about the entire saga."

"Why, whatever do you mean by that, my dear fellow?" I asked.

"A curious mystery surrounds the death of Irene Adler, Watson, and I am in the process of trying to unravel it."

He sat down in his armchair and once again scrutinized me with an impassioned intensity that unsettled me slightly.

"You see, I attended her funeral last Friday. That is to say, I had every intention of paying my last respects to the good lady. I took the train to Ramsgate. But when I arrived at the church at the allotted time,

I could find no evidence of a service. I was not alone in my disappointment, Watson. Several other persons had come to pay their respects and were similarly bewildered."

"What a confounded nuisance, Holmes!"

"And to cap it all, as I was leaving the churchyard, a young man in a heavy trench coat tipped his hat and greeted me with a 'Good day, Mr. Holmes.' I thought to myself, 'Now who the deuce was that?' As far as I knew, I had no close acquaintances in this part of Kent. Unless, of course, it was the son of a local bee-keeper who might have recognized me from my annual visits to the Canterbury regatta. I know nothing of the man except that he is fond of fox hunting and is a great disappointment to his father."

"I smell a rotten fish here, Holmes, and I rather think Mr. Godfrey Norton has something to do with it. I never did trust the man, to speak the truth, especially after he eloped with Miss Adler to the Continent. I fear that he may now be covering up some foul deed that he perpetrated on the innocent lady in some fit of jealous rage or the like."

"Yes, Watson, there might be some weight to your supposition." He paused thoughtfully. "For when I returned home later that day, there was a note waiting with my housekeeper. Here it is! Read it and please let me know your thoughts."

He handed me the note. It was on blue bonded vellum and typed in bold print. I read it aloud: "'Dear Mr. Holmes: My wife's recent death has convinced me of the need to return certain items of hers to rightful owners. She often apprised me of a photograph featuring her and the King of Bohemia that you desired with some urgency at one time. I would be happy to hand it over to you personally, if you would care to meet me at the Diogenes Club of Pall Mall on March 23 at 10.30 a.m. I remain your humble servant, Gordon Norton, Temple Inn.'"

I looked up. "Surely, you're not thinking of going, Holmes! Why, this could be a trap! There's no telling what the rascal might be planning. Some kind of blackmail, no doubt."

"I have my reasons for believing that there is more to this case than meets the eye, Watson. I grant you, it is always dangerous to speculate on inadequate information. But, for once, I am prepared to follow my heart and not my head. I do, indeed, desire that photograph and fully intend to acquire it."

"Then you shall not go alone. I intend to come along with you. That is, if you will permit me to do so."

Indeed, I felt it a great honor to be able to serve my distinguished companion in this, his time of dire need. And I sensed that, though he may not have admitted it, this was in fact the reason why I had been summoned from London in the first place.

□□□□□

The following Wednesday, at ten o'clock precisely, we met at Charing Cross station. From there, we shared a hansom cab to the Diogenes Club on the Strand, arriving punctually at 10:25 with five minutes to spare before our assigned rendezvous.

Clearly, powerful emotions had begun to stir once again in my esteemed friend. It would appear that whatever residue of feeling he might have harbored for Miss Adler had now mixed with a profound ambivalence about returning to the hurly-burly of London life. Indeed, I feared that the excitement of our current adventure might possibly disturb his delicate metabolism and throw him back into a sullen state of deep melancholia. With this in mind, I was doubly determined to keep him out of harm's way if at all humanly possible.

Our shared anxiety level was palpable, and I sensed that matters were about to get worse. Indeed, as we sat waiting on a leather sofa in the Lounge Room of the club, a familiar figure approached us menacingly. It was Holmes's elder brother, Mycroft, a regular patron of the establishment.

"Why, Sherlock, what a pleasant surprise!" he declared in a gravelly voice that seemed to carry with it an unmistakable hint of mockery. "It must be several years since you set foot inside our club. What could possibly bring you out of your blissful shell?" He pulled a thick cigar from a silver case and waved it in the air, as if for amusement.

Mycroft was widely regarded as an eccentric genius. He owned an intellect which was the equivalent of his brother's, perhaps even superior in its own way. His mastery of dates and facts was unrivalled. Unfortunately, the relationship between the two brothers had become rather strained in recent years, and I was not alone in secretly hoping that they would sooner or later find a way to celebrate once again their extraordinary talents in a spirit of mutual toleration.

Holmes responded to his brother's sarcastic undertone with admirable professionalism. "Mycroft," he said, "I must in this instance ask for the utmost discretion from you. My good friend, Watson, and I are here strictly on a business matter that need be of no concern to you at this time."

"I see!" replied Mycroft, clearing his throat, obviously relishing the aura of mystery that had suddenly been created.

"At any moment," Holmes continued, "we are expecting a client who will no doubt reveal himself to us and ..."

"But my dear chap," Mycroft interrupted. "I fear you may be too late! You see, I was handed this letter fifteen minutes ago and as it was addressed to "Mr. Holmes Esquire," I opened it. Naturally, I was somewhat puzzled by its contents. Here, see for yourselves."

I was able to study the note as it changed hands. In bold capitals, it said: "WHAT THING IS IT THAT WOMMEN MOOST DESIREN?" And then scrawled underneath, "Please bring your answer tomorrow at noon to Primrose Hill where I shall be at your disposal."

There appeared to be no signature or any trace that might indicate the author's identity.

"Another one of Norton's tricks, perhaps?" I scoffed. "But what on earth does it mean?"

Holmes seemed all of a sudden to regain his alertness. "I believe we are close to finding out, Watson!" he said with a trace of excitement. "Mycroft, I must make immediate use of the library here. Please tell me where I might locate a compendium of medieval literature."

"Why certainly, Sherlock. I would be delighted to assist you in this matter. In fact," he smiled, lighting his cigar ceremoniously, "I can save you a lot of time and bother. Please wait here while I retrieve the book you require."

He returned shortly, carrying a leather-bound copy of Geoffrey Chaucer's *The Canterbury Tales*. He had opened it to a page in *The Wife of Bath's Tale* and was pointing at it with a self-congratulatory smile on his face. "Here, I believe, is the passage you are looking for."

Holmes studied the lines, frowning with intense concentration. His frown quickly gave way to a look of elation such as I had seen in my good friend on those rare occasions when the mysteries of the universe are suddenly fathomed.

"By Jove, I think I've got it!" he thundered. He stood up abruptly and clasped Mycroft's hand. "My dear brother, irrespective of my recent frostiness towards you, I have always admired the manner in which you used your considerable talent on behalf of His Majesty's government. Likewise, I thank you for now casting light on a matter that is somewhat closer to my heart."

Mycroft appeared taken aback by his brother's burst of personal commendation. "Yes, quite so, Sherlock," he muttered while stubbing out his cigar.

I was, frankly, at sixes and sevens. But after many years working alongside Holmes, I had grown accustomed to being in the company of a man whose mind worked at a swifter speed than any other person I had ever known.

Holmes continued: "Well, gentlemen, we have one more piece of the puzzle to solve and that can wait until tomorrow. In the meantime, I would be delighted to share your company. Mycroft, perhaps we might catch up on our news and share a warm toddy together?"

Not wishing to intrude further on the scene, I decided to make my apologies and return home to my good wife. But before I departed, Holmes insisted that I meet him on the following day at Primrose Hill so as to witness the encounter with Norton which promised to close the case once and for all.

□□□□□□

In all of my adventures with Sherlock Holmes, I have rarely witnessed such strange proceedings as took place on top of Primrose Hill the next day.

It was a splendid spring morning. Many Londoners were out and about, enjoying the gentle breezes and soft sunshine. Unfortunately, Holmes and I were prevented from partaking in such simple pleasures, as we were determined to stick to the business at hand.

I was instructed by my friend to stand back at a distance of thirty or forty paces so as not to interfere with proceedings. I duly staked my ground behind an elm tree which offered suitable coverage, and then watched eagerly as the anticipated meeting between Holmes and

Newton came to pass.

It reminded me of an encounter between two duelists in full regalia. Holmes had disguised himself as some sort of non-conformist clergyman with a broad black hat and dark baggy trousers. Norton, for his part, was heavily draped in an all-black mourning costume. They circled around one another for some time before eventually drawing closer. I assumed the crouch position, poised to intervene at a moment's notice in the event of a sudden physical altercation. But rather than trade blows, they appeared to exchange words amicably and then exchanged small packages. Moments later, they shook hands. It was a somewhat protracted handshake, I felt.

I began to wonder what these two were up to. I had expected a physical tussle between two rivals but, in truth, the whole affair was fast becoming a pantomime spectacle more worthy of Puss in Boots. The pair continued to tarry further in this frolicsome manner before finally parting ways. Norton turned to walk down the hill towards Regent's Park with a distinctive spring in his step.

Holmes gave me the all-clear signal and I sprang out of the shade of the tree and paced briskly over to meet my friend. He seemed flushed and excited, and was breathing rather heavily.

"Well, Holmes, what on earth was that all about?" I inquired.

"I believe, Watson, I have just killed two birds with one stone." He smiled and pointed to the receding figure of Godfrey Norton continuing down the pathway.

"Behold the resurrected Irene Adler," he announced. "A woman whose wit and beauty will forever reside close to my heart."

"Good gracious! Surely, you can't be serious?" I focused on the figure in the distance. "I mean how is that humanly possible, Holmes?"

"It is as elementary as solving a well composed riddle, my dear friend. And in this case, I was both the subject and object of the riddle. Once again, I have been outplayed by a woman's wit!"

I was, at this stage, feeling utterly perplexed about the whole affair. "I assume this has got something to do with that confounded question concerning the wants and desires of the fairer sex?"

"Indeed, Watson. And the answer to that question, so ably provided to me by my brother, is, to use Geoffrey Chaucer's expression, 'sovereynetee.'"

"Meaning what, in heaven's name?"

"Authority, mastery, control, the ability to move and manipulate others. In short, the power of wit and cunning! Mycroft was able to provide the answer by referring to *The Wife of Bath's Tale*. But it was Miss Adler herself who was able to demonstrate it a few minutes ago when I was outwitted by her in no uncertain terms."

"Holmes, it is very unlike you to concede defeat in such a humbling manner. Are you sure you are quite well?"

"Perfectly well, thank you, Watson. You need have no fear. Now, come let us descend the hill and I will reveal all to you in due course."

We remained silent for a period of time as we started to follow the footpath down the hill towards Regent's Park. Finally, I broke the silence.

"Tell me, Holmes. How long had you suspected that Irene Adler was still alive?"

"Suspicion is one thing, Watson. Knowledge is an entirely different proposition. I suspected that she might still be alive after I undertook my futile journey to Ramsgate. But I did not know it as a fact until I saw her in person, albeit heavily disguised as a man."

"Yes, but why on earth did she resort to such an elaborate costume?"

"An excellent question, my dear fellow, for which I can only hazard a guess based on an understanding of my own motives. For surely you could have directed a similar inquiry at me? She and I are, in many ways, perfectly aligned. She remains a mistress of disguise after her distinguished career as an opera singer. As for myself, I am a dabbler in disguise because of my love for solving crimes. A few minutes ago, I recognized her and she obviously recognized me, but we observed strict protocol in carrying out our business transaction."

"Do you mean that you never exposed yourself to her, or confessed your deep admiration for her?"

"Good God, no! That simply wouldn't be playing by the rules of the game, Watson. The encounter was, as I said, strictly professional. I answered the riddle and she rewarded me with the highly desirable photograph of her that I sought all along."

"And what did you give her in return?"

He smiled and answered: "Ah, that is my secret, Watson. There are some parts of my being to which I will not allow even you, my closest confidante, to gain access."

I chuckled, content in this piece of knowledge, and felt privileged that once again, I had been privy to a profound mystery that had been probed to its fullest capacity and resolved in a most just and satisfactory manner.

But as we approached the bottom of the hill, I was suddenly struck by another unanswered question. "I say, Holmes. How do you account for the obituary and the funeral announcement?"

"Well, it appears that she knew me better than I thought. Clearly, she was aware of my daily habit of reading *The Times*. A well-placed announcement in the "Death Notices" column was guaranteed to lure me out of retirement. Once I had taken the bait, you see, she was able once again to enjoy complete mastery over me. The appearance of the gentleman at the church burial, who bid me good-day, was simply another clever act. Indeed, it was the same ploy that she had used in the Bohemian case. On that occasion, Watson, as you may recall, she dressed up in a similar costume and offered an identical greeting outside my Baker Street lodging."

"I see," I said, not entirely certain whether I should be in awe of the woman's cleverness or critical of her wily deceptions.

Holmes continued: "And then, of course, there was the business of being invited to Mycroft's club at a time of the day when, as she was well aware, my brother is habitually in attendance. Of course, being the learned book man that he is, Mycroft was able to crack the literary clue with admirable alacrity. Indeed, I began to detect a convergence of clues that would eventually lead to our final encounter on Primrose Hill. As to the riddle itself, from England's great medieval poet, I surmised it would take a woman of the arts to employ it, not a man of the law such as Godfrey Norton whose literary tastes are typically more direct and circumscribed."

After a pause, he resumed: "Besides, Norton and she were legally separated three years ago, as I recall, and therein lies another similarity between Miss Adler and the Wife of Bath. However," he quickly added, "I don't believe she has remarried four times! She is quite a woman, Watson. And I'd be the first to admit that, in this case, she has provided an almost perfect demonstration of the long-lost art of feminine 'sovereynetee.'"

"Yes, I dare say! And now she's gone away. Probably back to New York where, no doubt, she will delight in telling stories about the two occasions in her life when she outwitted the most famous detective that London has ever known!"

I noticed a sardonic smile on Holmes's face as he stopped in his tracks and said, "Please spare me such accolades, my dear fellow! And remember that I am, after all, officially retired from my past practice. These last few days have been quite a strain on my nerves. I intend to return at once to my home in the Sussex countryside where I can continue to dabble in the delights and mysteries of bee-keeping. Such daily demands will suffice to keep me away from further distractions of the heart, I assure you."

My Insufferable Nemesis

We have unmistakeable proof that throughout all past time, there has been a ceaseless devouring of the weak by the strong

[Herbert Spencer]

If you happen to find yourself on top of Parliament Hill, be sure to stop and admire the view of London's famous landmarks laid out before you. On a clear day, you might see as far as Canary Wharf or possibly the Houses of Parliament shimmering in the distance. As you stand there taking in the sights, you'll no doubt feel a powerful breeze tug at your overcoat and hear the rustling of leaves from a cluster of oak trees halfway down the hill. You'll turn to look and your attention will be drawn to a prominent green dome on the opposite side of the hill. Adjacent to this dome, out of view, is Highgate Cemetery East.

Here, in plot fifty-four, is where my remains are to be found.

I see that I have commanded your attention. Perhaps, therefore, you will allow me to guide you towards my resting place and share the story of my insufferable nemesis along the way?

First, let us descend the hill, keeping to the main pathway. Notice this wooden bench with the inscribed dedication, "Phillip Brainwhite (1832–1888): a Kindly Man and Noble Citizen." Yes, Brainwhite was a loyal friend, a fellow sociologist who embodied the best of British intellectual traditions. He and I both resented the continental philosophers of the day whose flowery idealism had become too fashionable for our more prosaic tastes.

For twenty-seven years, Brainwhite unfailingly walked his whippets on Hampstead Heath before breakfast. After he died from tuberculosis, I commissioned the bench to be erected in his honor. It was the honorable thing to do for a man who derived so much pleasure from the heath. Altruism, he and I agreed, was the highest form of human behavior and a source of intense personal happiness. Indeed, we both believed that self-sacrifice for the common good was the key to human survival and prosperity. Alas, you won't find such noble sentiments in the work of my nemesis.

But I am jumping ahead of myself. Please excuse my excessive fervor.

We must now fork left and follow the footpath away from the Heath, past Kathy's Tea-room, and into Highgate Village. Let us exit here into Swains Lane. Notice the flurry of middle-class establishments—a floral shop, a newsagent, a computer store, a hairdresser, even a continental café. Spurred on by keen economic competition, these shops seem to change hands every two or three years, a trend which might disgruntle those with nostalgic leanings but is, I believe, in conformity with the simplest law of human nature: the survival of the fittest. Indeed, as I argued in my groundbreaking book, *First Principles*, there is unmistakable proof that throughout time, the weak have always been devoured by the strong. This theory I held to be as true for the marketplace as it was for the school playground or the rugby pitch.

The condition of the houses further along Swains Lane proves my point perfectly. Note well this row of modern semi-detached homes with ornate front gardens bordered by neatly-trimmed privet hedges. I believe that the immaculate order of these homesteads helps to explain the political and economic success of the middle classes. "Hats off to them," that's what I say.

Now, see there, on the opposite side of the road, a collection of Victorian gothic buildings topped with stacked chimneys and slanting rooflines. Notice the cracked stucco and missing slate shingles on many of the houses. It saddens me to observe how their grandeur has declined over the years. Nevertheless, regrettable as it may be, the process is inevitable and there's nothing one can do to stem natural decay.

The lane takes a turn at this juncture as we begin our gradual ascent to Highgate Cemetery. On our left is Holly Lodge Housing Estate, a curious mixture of modern council flats and neo-Tudor maisonettes. Frankly, I abhor this hodgepodge of contrasting styles. It reminds me of King's Cross railway station, built to great acclaim in the middling years of my life, and ceremonially opened by Queen Victoria in 1851. Of course, the popular press perceived it as an historic bridge between high and low culture. However, in my opinion, it was nothing more than an overindulgent façade disguising an inner mediocrity. If civilization is to strive towards a higher unity of truth and principle, I argued at the time, one comes to expect a certain consistency of tastes and values. Otherwise, where is the common consensus? Where is our vision of a shared culture?

I hear my nemesis mock these sentiments. I can hear him laughing now.

"Ah, my good fellow," he sneers in pronounced Teutonic tones. "Your faith in human progress is much overvalued. Why do you waste your time examining the stucco that covers the bricks of our social institutions? Look instead at the cracks beneath the surface, my friend, for it is the cracks that reveal more about the weak foundation of a building. Diagnose the strains and tensions of society, not the surface appearance."

Then his voice is gone, spirited away.

Yet be aware of his mocking tones as I guide you closer to my resting place. And try not to be swayed, as so many others were, by his mesmerizing charm and seductive continental accent.

□□□□□

Oh yes, I knew him in my day. It was impossible to ignore his meteoric rise to fame, especially after his much-heralded move to London in 1848. He gained a reputation for his ritual visits to the Reading Room of the British Museum where he developed his infamous theory about the law of surplus value. It was, he boasted, a revolutionary theory grounded equally in idealism and hard empiricism. To be stuck exclusively in either one was to ignore the dynamic of the dialectic, he claimed. By inference, I was typecast as a reactionary apologist for unfettered capitalism.

His adversarial stance towards my theories of natural selection became progressively uncharitable. It started with the publication of a letter he wrote to *The Economist,* translated from German by his associate, Mr. Engels. The letter assailed the philosophical basis of my life's work. The year was 1853. I was, at the time, sub-editor of that leading journal and had commissioned a series of articles by like-minded colleagues on the value of laissez-faire economic theory. We propounded that society was evolving from a state of immaturity to a state of perfection and happiness, governed principally by the fundamental quality of altruism. The agents of this radical transformation were the middling ranks of society, who were suitably educated and responsible to do the bidding on behalf of human civilization.

In his reproving letter, he wrote: "I share with my esteemed colleague his profound hopes and ideals for the future of humanity. But, it appears that I am destined to play the role of his nemesis. I look to the day when all men, irrespective of class or caste, will be able to hunt in the morning, fish in the afternoon, and criticize after dinner without ever becoming hunter, fisherman, or critic by trade. However, in order to attain such a classless society, a supreme sacrifice is required from those classes in whose interest it is to maintain the status quo. The belief that our society is progressing organically towards a state of perfection is nothing more than the abstract theory of a seriously flawed mind."

☐☐☐☐☐

Initially, I was perturbed by the vigor of his attack. I felt somewhat like a pugilist who had been knocked to the canvas. Yet, I knew I possessed the strength and inner belief to regain my footing and continue with the contest. I was convinced, after all, that his brand of continental philosophy would never adapt successfully to the soils of England fertilized by the virtues of decency, honor, and tradition.

Indeed, it dawned on me that I had made a sworn enemy for life. I remember the exact time and place when the full impact of this realization struck home. It was during a meeting of the Athenaeum Club's Great Ideas Committee on January 16, 1860. I feel compelled to recall the event now as we conclude our walk together.

Several Fellows of the Royal Society and their guests, including Charles Darwin, had been invited to discuss the merits of the Welfare State in response to Darwin's recent postulations in his controversial volume, *On the Origin of Species*. Thomas Huxley was the first to address the assembly and wasted no time in condemning "the cult of fanatical individualism" that, he attributed to Darwin and me.

"Let me appeal to all that is ethically best in human nature," Huxley reasoned from the podium. "Instead of ruthless self-assertion, a society demands self-restraint. Laws and moral precepts should remind us of our duty to the community so that we elevate ourselves beyond that of a brute savage."

Huxley, as usual, sounded reasonable and convincing. But I was swift to counter his argument by insisting that the welfare state threatened the evolutionary process. Natural selection, I pointed out, was a method for weeding out the wasteful elements, the chaff, of our society.

I continued: "There must exist in our midst a certain amount of misery. This is the normal result of misconduct and misery ought not to be dissociated from it. Welfare legislation, I submit, merely prevents evolution by removing the incentive for each individual to adapt himself to the social state."

I felt that my comments had been suitably forceful and persuasive. Huxley seemed strangely quiet as if defeated by the brilliant logic of my argument. I noticed Darwin in the far corner of the smoking-room talking animatedly with a gentleman in an armchair whose back was turned away from me. I could only see the thick cigar smoke billowing from the chair and the top of the gentleman's thick grey hair. I have to admit, I felt a deep sense of triumph at that moment. I had, after all, engaged in a vigorous debate with the finest minds of our land on an issue of current and vital importance. And not only had I held my own; I was convinced I had won the day.

Imagine my surprise, therefore, when a few minutes later, upon settling into my favorite settee, and striking up a conversation with a prominent barrister, a private note was delivered to me on a silver tray. It was on a plain card. Scrawled in bold capital letters were the words: "BOSH AND POPPYCOCK! YOUR MIND IS AS FLAWED AS EVER." It was signed, "Your Nemesis."

I cannot begin to explain the sheer effrontery of the man.

Sadly, it was typical of the cavalier behavior I came to expect from him. It became part of his ongoing campaign to deride my life's work. In response, I attempted to retain the dignified demeanor befitting a person of my pedigree. Consequently, upon his death in 1883, I decided to suspend our hostilities and pay homage to his career in a letter to *The Times*. I praised his robust intellect yet pointed out that, in the final analysis, it was not suited to an English temperament weathered by soft drizzle and gentle mists.

Twenty years later, as I lay on my deathbed, I felt confident that my legacy would endure for years to come and that the works of my nemesis would diminish in importance as a matter of course.

Why, then, am I to be found wide awake in the afterlife, pacing back and forth along these streets, pulling bystanders like yourself along the way?

We are drawing closer to the source of my unease.

□□□□□

Here, at the entrance to Highgate Cemetery East, you pay a small contribution to the lady at the gate. For this fee, you enter a world of spirits and ghosts, most sleeping peacefully in perennial slumber while others, like me, remain desperately awake. Let us proceed past the Dalziel Mausoleum and the Polish corner, noticing the broken columns and Celtic crosses along the way. At the first junction, we fork left and walk fifty paces before arriving at plot number fifty-four. It is a simple tomb made of dark granite. On it is the inscription: "*Herbert* Spencer *(1820–1903): Philosopher and Pioneer of Sociology in Britain.*"

This is my resting place.

You'll notice the area around the tomb has been left to ruin in a state of natural decay. After all, who has the inclination to look after it or offer a helping hand these days? Who even knows that I inhabit this place now that holly and creeping ivy have almost entirely covered my epitaph?

As you stand there absorbing such questions, you will soon register the reason for my agony and lasting spiritual torment. Directly opposite, there stands a monolithic slab of stone, famous the world over as the bust of my sworn enemy, Karl Marx. Notice the way he looks at my tomb with scorn and mockery. Notice, in particular, the confident smirk.

For half a century, I inhabited this corner of the cemetery in peace, surrounded by cultured souls of gentle persuasion. But then, in the mid-1950s, cemetery wardens decided to relocate the body of my nemesis here, along with his wife and progeny. They proceeded to erect this larger-than-life bronze monument of the bearded revolutionary, giving it that distinctive smirk fraught with aggressive self-confidence.

Underneath his bust are words that prick my soul: *"The Philosophers have only interpreted the world in various ways. The point however is to change it."*

Am I to take this personally? Am I to consider that my lifelong quest to explain the workings of human civilization was simply a futile exercise in interpretation? A waste of time? Is this why my endeavors have been overlooked in the modern age while my nemesis has attained cult status?

Once again, please forgive my fervor. I did not bring you here to listen to the ranting of a disillusioned man. Yet, I have borne sad witness to the horrible human destruction committed in the name of Marxist class struggles throughout the twentieth century. The ideology has spawned monsters like Lenin, Stalin, Mao, and Pol Pot. The combined legacies of such charlatans must surely repel any freethinker worth their salt. And in recognition of such an unassailable fact, isn't this why the Berlin Wall crumbled? Isn't this why the Cold War came to its inevitable conclusion with the collapse of the Soviet empire? And isn't this why capitalism, in its benevolent form, has finally prevailed across the globe?

Why, then, must I endure such shameful neglect in the shadow of my nemesis?

Daily, I am reminded that my work and reputation have frittered away. Every rose that is laid at his headstone, every photograph that is taken of his grave site, every group of tourists that hovers excitedly around his statue, compound my eternal agony. I hear his spirit shout out in mocking tones, *"Ah, Spencer, my dear fellow! Wie gehts, eh?"* And then I imagine one of his eyes winking at me in a gesture of brazen impudence.

No wonder you find me today, a restless spirit, calling out for comfort and support from sympathetic passers-by like yourself.

Yet I refuse to become an extinct species. Indeed, I am convinced that my period of intellectual exile will soon end, and that Marx's reputation as a social prophet shall be smashed to pieces. It's a question of matter and motion. The belief in pure evolution spearheaded by me, along with Charles Darwin and others, shall return to favor, and the Marxist curse of class warfare will be cast off forever.

And on that day, you will return to Parliament Hill and you will discover that the usual collection of kite flyers, joggers, and dog owners are fraternizing freely. A profound sense of harmony and well-being will sweep over you. For you'll recognize that this glorious vision is the consequence of ideals that I, Herbert Spencer, propagated in a lifetime devoted to the free market economy. At last, my faith in unfettered capitalism and the survival of the fittest shall have won the day.

To achieve this vision and bring about the downfall of my nemesis along with everything he stands for, may I count on your help and intervention? Perhaps, even, a smattering of altruism?

The Purest Ecstasy

The beauty of the world has two edges, one of laughter, one of anguish, cutting the heart asunder

[Virginia Woolf]

Once again, the lonely avenue stretches in front of me. I have walked it countless times, and have taken comfort in its succession of statuettes, tazzas, and flowerbeds. As always, Chester Road will serve as a natural divide between my Voyage Out and Voyage In. Beyond this threshold, I know that I will be pulled past the wolf cages of London Zoo to the end of Regent's Park.

But what will be my end?

Where did I—Adeline Virginia Stephen—begin?

As usual, I begin my promenade by crossing Marylebone Road and leave the clatter of Bloomsbury behind. I am here at the Broadwalk Gate at a quarter to three on this Sunday afternoon in early March 1941. The air is damp and cold; thick clouds scud across the sky. I am wearing white gloves, a dark overcoat, and field-boots. Around me, the parade of humanity streams along the Broadwalk.

I see a toddler in bright red Wellington boots leaping gleefully after fattened pigeons. A tall, smartly-dressed gentleman strides homeward, possibly from church or a rendezvous with a secret paramour. There are stories to be mined here, of a Hugh, a Ralph, or a Lucy. But I cannot afford to lose myself in their ordinary lives and become weightless again. For too long, I have abandoned myself to the lives of others. Today, I must face myself undisguised and unprotected. I must create a narrative shape for my own life.

And so I start with a reminiscence of our family holiday in Cornwall when I was eleven years old. From the bedroom window of our summer home I could hear the sea weaves breaking, one-two, one-two, crashing onto the beach below. I immersed myself in a world of fantasy and make-believe, of romance and derring-do. In my mind's eye, I sailed out of St. Ives harbor, bobbing slowly into a misty expanse of air and water. I was a sea-maiden calling out to passing ships, luring sailors to their early deaths.

These dreamscapes afford me the purest ecstasy.

I remember that my elder sister, Nessa, and I were building sand barriers on the beach as the tide came in. A distant voice from the sea startled me.

"Follow me," the voice beckoned.

I turned and saw a light blinking on and off beyond the rocks. "Follow me," the voice persisted.

As I faced the open sea, I wanted to merge with my surroundings and lose myself altogether. My sister lunged towards me, her hands covered with muddy sand.

"Come on, goat!" she taunted. "Let's get to work. We'll never hold back the water at this rate."

I dug out a glob of wet sand with my shovel and packed it down on the wall that we had built. But it seemed we were losing our battle against the sea, for the wall began to sink as eddies of water started to spill over. I marveled at the power of the water and thrilled to the sound of the voice that was calling me from far away.

"Well, that's the end of that," Nessa said sternly. "Come on, I'll race you back." Further along the beach, Mother and Father sat in their deck chairs behind a windbreak, sipping tea. Father, dressed in white flannel trousers and collarless shirt, was reading his beloved volume of Gibbon. Mother, cheerful and gay in her striped silk dress, was making marmite sandwiches. Both seemed solid and stable in that frozen moment, quite oblivious to the battle between sea and sand raging around them. In my mind, they remain there to this day, a permanent fixture on the Cornish sands.

"Girls, come and have your sandwiches!" Mother commanded musically. I still sense the softness of her voice forty years later, mixed with the taste of marmite, the sharpness of sea-salt air, and the briny smell of seaweed.

But the moment was suddenly interrupted by the irrepressible Vanessa.

"Follow me!" she barked. And I bounded after her, ready to chase her to the end of the beach, to the end of the world if necessary.

It is as if we existed in a bubble, and life's joys—walking, picking flowers, talking, reading—could be sealed inside the bubble and made to last forever. It was in that self-enclosed space where only our voices could be heard, punctuated by others from the outside world on the rarest of occasions.

But when Mother passed away on May 5, 1895, the bubble burst open.

"Hold yourself straight, my little goat," she told me, as she lay dying in the upstairs bedroom. I was hopeless at heeding her advice.

Now, as I approach Chester Road, my walk is predictably interrupted. Other pedestrians have stopped ahead of me and wait at the curbside for passing motorcars and omnibuses to clear. I know that once I cross this road, I will never be the same again. It is an undisputed fact that nothing remains stable for long. Once I cross this road, I must replay a scene that lurks in my memory as an unwanted presence. It assails my thoughts at unbidden moments. Inevitably, it returns to me now.

I was in the dank, gloomy house at Hyde Park Gate. Vanessa and I had returned from a soiree where we had played the part of bohemian debutantes with customary aplomb.

Cigar smoke hung to our clothes and brandy coursed through our blood. George Duckworth had performed his customary role of protective half-brother by reprimanding Vanessa and me for our lack of social decorum around people of power and high position. We felt suitably admonished and humbled.

I was in bed. The lights were out. The house was silent, funereal in fact, as Father had been taken seriously ill and, for the previous fortnight, had been confined to the spare room downstairs.

There was a tap on the door. Then it opened. The floorboard creaked, and a shaft of light fell on a shadowy face.

"Who's there?" I cried.

I could distinguish the muttonchop sideburns of my half-brother.

"Don't be frightened," he whispered hoarsely as he lurched un-evenly towards my bed. "And don't turn on the light, my beloved." I could feel the sharp sting of his alcohol- breath on my face. Then he wrapped his arms around my body and started to kiss my forehead.

I stiffened, hoping he would stop. Instead, his hands groped under the bedclothes, going steadily lower. I struggled but he did not stop. He explored, as if fully licensed to roam at will.

Then he whispered softly into my hair, "Poor father. Hush now, dearest. You must take care of yourself. Fear no more."

He held my head to his chest and stroked my hair gently. "Tush! Tush! My little one." Then he slipped off the bed and walked out of the room, taking with him my innocence and the easy gaiety that had been bestowed on me by a long line of ancestresses.

Never were we to talk of those irreversible moments. I was left with an utterly loathsome feeling that my world would never belong to me again; rather, it would be possessed by another, by "him." Thereafter, I was doomed to take the path home, the Voyage In.

Everything, ultimately, is brought back to physical touch and the material nature of things.

I remember waking up later that night and being horribly aware that, down below, Father was dying of cancer.

◻◻◻◻◻

After Chester Road, the landscape of the park changes drastically. Cultivated flower beds give way to an expansive heath dotted with elm and sycamore trees.

My life at its midpoint endured similar transformations. I had lost both my parents. My sister and I lived in a conspiracy of silence with our half-brother. Comfort came from Thursday soirees when, over hot currant buns and cigarettes, our circle of bohemians delighted in con-versations about beauty and truth, the pure ecstasy of intellect and spirit. I remember Strachey pointing his walking stick at a soap stain on my dress.

"What have we got here?" he asked in a mock-stern tone of voice. "Semen?" We burst into laughter at the thought of such an immaculate conception.

We were trying to fabricate a world of ethereal beauty in spite of our drab surroundings. But George Duckworth insisted that we inhabit what he called the real world and become more involved in current affairs like the crisis in South Africa, the decline of the Liberal Party, and the problem of tramcar congestion in the West End.

I was hopeless at that kind of worldly banter. Whenever I tried, I felt like a fly stuck in a pot of glue. At a Gower dinner party once, the conversation turned to Empire and its virtues. Major Roger Crenshaw, from the India Regiment, was guest of honor at the gathering, organized by the imperious Lady Ottoline. Her idea of enlightened repartee was the very antithesis of our spontaneous Bloomsbury conversations.

I remember her nasal, sing-songy pontification that evening. "One of the great thrills about serving in the colonies," she chimed, "must be the sheer power it gives you, as a military leader, over others, don't you agree Roger?"

Vanessa bristled. "What do you mean by 'others'?" she asked.

"You know! Other 'types,'" Lady Ottoline recurred.

"Well, yes, I suppose you could say that," the Major hesitated, nervously fingering his cheese knife as he talked. "Actually, I don't give it too much consideration. My main job, after all, is to serve King and Country."

"Quite right, Major," George added. "It is our duty to provide the benefits of civilization to our colonies, rather than become embroiled in questions of power and mastery."

I must have chortled conspicuously at this last remark for George suddenly turned to me and said, "Well, Virginia, what do you think?"

A table of faces stared at me. Inside my head, a thousand voices seemed to speak at the same time and I blurted, "Where is the Holy Ghost in all of this?"

There was an uneasy silence. Then my half-brother said sarcastically, "Where, indeed, Virginia? Where, indeed?" And he gave me a look that was clearly intended to shred me to pieces.

My life breaks down at this juncture. I approach a puddle in the middle of the avenue but I cannot step across it. I simply cannot proceed further. Menacing voices inside my head mix with the distant sounds of traffic. A meadowlark sings of death and immortality. Tree branches wave furiously at me.

I rest on a bench.

By withdrawing so deeply into myself, I realize how I have become hopelessly disconnected from others. The whole world seems engaged in the ordinary pleasures of life while I am ruled by a mind that explodes with ceaseless noise.

"Yet beauty is everywhere!" I cry out loud as if to reassure myself. "I must grasp it!" A stranger approaches and asks, "Excuse me, do you have the time?"

He points emphatically at his wrist. "The time?" he persists.

It returns me to a world of clocks and mechanical regularity. I fumble inside my coat pocket and take out the stopwatch given to me by Leonard, marked with the inscription "To V.S. from L.W."

"Ah, dear, dear man!" I murmur.

There is a cough. The stranger is lingering, waiting for his answer. "Why, it is already a quarter past three!"

The words ring like solid chimes and the man disappears from my consciousness. I am reminded that I too have enjoyed my share of simple pleasures and ordinary moments. And for this I have to thank my faithful husband, Leonard. I can see him now: his tall, thin frame, his powerful blue eyes, his mouth shaped into a sardonic smile. And I can hear his gravelly voice measuring out words with scientific precision.

"I think, my love" he enunciates carefully, "that we need to draw up a contract in which we delineate a program of rest and recovery."

And so, as the world went to war in 1914, he and I signed our peace treaty. I was to drink one glass of milk in the morning, rest for an hour and a half after luncheon, take beef tea and cod liver oil in the late afternoon, followed by a light supper of haddock and sausage before going to bed by ten o'clock without fail.

We sought refuge in Monk's House deep in the Sussex countryside. There, we took comfort in the pleasures of a calm routine: pruning the rhododendrons, walking the dogs by the river, and reading in the sun parlor. At the end of the day, Leonard's calm, kind voice soothed my spirits. At night, in bed, his arm draped lightly over my waist.

In this atmosphere of peace and quiet, I enjoyed the daily practice of writing. Mysterious voices, bidden and unbidden, called to me. I wrote at breakneck speed, knowing that if the feeling were lost, so too would the moment of absolute authenticity, the essential thing itself. I poured myself into acts of creation, losing myself in the other, and the about-to-be-created.

When it was all done and the story successfully brought to fruition, I was broken, exhausted, spent. There was nothing left in me. At those moments, I would feel a sharp pain, like a fin in the water slicing across my body. I dreaded the vacuum between acts of literary creation. I called it "dead space" and I feared plunging into its unwelcome waters. The only remedy was to return to the chatter and social excitement of Bloomsbury: the highbrow parties at Tavistock Square, the West End theatres, the book club gatherings.

Thus we endured our cycle of pain and pleasure through the years.

□□□□□

I get up from the bench. My legs are weary and my mind darkens, like the skies above me. The final stretch of the walk will take me past the cages of London Zoo to the Outer Circle, and then over the bridge that crosses the Cumberland Basin of Regent's Canal. The savage howl of Hitler's war rages in the background. Its air-raid sirens and explosions invade this body, this human frame, walking along the Broadwalk at half past three on a Sunday afternoon.

I am overwhelmed by questions. How can I contribute to the war effort? How can I be of use? What determination can I discover in myself to keep me going to the end? Is it possible during this time of war to keep calm detachment? To stem acedia, the sin of gloominess and despondency?

And who is this waiting for me on the bridge at the end of my walk? What shape is this? The cut of his coat is stern but proper. He leans on a walking stick. His back is turned to me as he looks down into the water.

I know this shape and demeanor. Now he turns but I cannot see the whole face, only the lips of his mouth opening and forming words.

"Follow me," he says.

I draw closer to the voice.

Is it Leonard? Dear, dear Leonard. I have cherished a lasting happiness with you. You have always been such a gentle, loving, and understanding man married to a woman who, for most of her life, has been swept along by a current of dark despair.

"Leonard!" I cry out. "Oh dearest, I am so afraid. I think I am going under again." I increase my pace. "Shall we try once again to defeat this horror, darling?"

I cross the road and reach the bridge. "Is it you, my love?"

He turns. I recognize the thick moustache, creased smile, and muttonchop sideburns. The voice says flatly, "Fear no more, my love. Tush! Tush!"

I shudder in horror as I draw alongside the figure of my half-brother on the bridge. I see shapes in the water below: hordes of women, my ancestresses. "Follow us," they beseech me.

"Nessa!" I cry out.

Now I understand how it will all end. I whisper to the shapes in the water: "Against you, death, I will fling myself, unvanquished and unyielding."

I plan my ending.

I will rise early at Monk's House and open the curtains without waking Leonard. I will pad down the stairs into the kitchen where I will prepare tea, two pieces of toast, and a boiled egg. I will read *The Times,* paying particular attention to the royal engagements and letters to the editor. I will write a note to Leonard: "I can't go on spoiling your life any longer. I don't think two people could have been happier than we have been. V."

I will place it next to the milk jug on the kitchen table. Later, he will take it next door and read it in the quiet emptiness of the living room. I will walk down the garden path, past the parish church and village hall, to the bank of the river. I will place two large stones in my coat-pockets.

Then I shall plunge into the water, into a jumbled memory of horror and delight—a splash of waves on a beach, the innocent laughter of a Bloomsbury soiree, a hand groping in the dark, a fin in the sea—and I shall go swiftly towards the light deep down inside.

Spirit Helpers

*Philip Clark, Plumber to this Collegiate
Church, b. 22nd. October 1664, d. 21st.
September 1707*

[Epitaph, West Cloister of Westminster Abbey]

My name is Phillip Clark and I am a spirit helper. That's right, I'm one of the chosen few who guide the lost and lonely with comforting caresses and cockney charisma.

You're probably thinking, "Codswallop! How come an ordinary bloke like yourself, a mere plumber for god's sake, carries out the Guv'nor's work instead of gaffers like Christopher bloody Wren or Oliver bleeding Cromwell?"

Now, I might appear like an ordinary bloke on the outside but, believe me, I'm capable of plumbing the deepest secrets of the universe. "Eternal rewards shall come to the virtuous," that's my creed. And that's why, on this dull and damp morning, it's me and my old mate, Tom Crapper, who are soaring high above the murky skyline of London Town, ready to go about our daily business tending to all the pitiful mortal souls down below.

"Behold the snaking curve of Mistress Thames, Tom" I marvel from on high. "Hark at the humanity surging across Westminster Bridge. Ain't you proud we're performing our celestial duties on such a glorious day, eh?"

Tom is not impressed by my palaver, which is fairly typical of the codger. "It's all a mess," he moans. "The pavements are littered with crap, the buildings are caked with grime, and those pathetic creatures down there look wet and miserable, if you ask me."

In truth, Tom has swallowed his zeal for the afterlife. In plain English, he's spent his spunk, murdered his mirth, and cobbled his kabul.

Don't get me wrong, it's not unusual for plumbers like me and Tom to be afflicted by a spot of pungent melancholia once we reach "the other side." After all, we gave the best years of our mortal lives to the fixing of pipes, urinals, and other sanitary devices. We waded in the mire, if you catch my drift.

Tom's case, however, takes the biscuit. The lad is well and truly down in the proverbial dumps and it's my job to fix him, once and for all, good and proper. "What's so special about me?" he yaps away. "Why have I been chosen to be a spirit helper, for god's sake?"

Right on cue, as we drift over Westminster Bridge, he carries on in that churlish tone of his: "Tell me, Phil. What did I contribute to human history? It's not as if I did anything spectacular like Christopher Wren. I was just an ordinary plumber going about my daily business."

"Not so ordinary, Tom," I reply. I try to keep a stoic face though it's a bit of a strain seeing as we've had this conversation countless times before.

Clearly, it's time for some of the old Level One treatment, soothing words of praise to lift his spirits. So I say, "You were one of the best, mate. Before you came along, think of the poor blighters who endured the Great Stink. Why, without your valve-less wastewater preventer or long-chained flush toilet, all those mortals would be rolling in their own muck to this very day."

We come to a halt on the bridge. Tom wears a rueful expression as if part of him wants to believe what I'm jabbering on about, while the other part is unconvinced.

"All right, I was a decent plumber," he says sheepishly. "But where's the honor in being remembered for flushing excrement down drainpipes? I mean, that's hardly enough to deserve celestial promotion, is it?"

"Ah, but the Guv'nor works in mysterious ways, Tom!" I hang an arm around his ethereal frame as we glide towards Whitehall. "You're soon to be His helper and it's not for us to reason why. After all, we're part of the chosen few, mate. Spirit helping is all about keeping the faith. Trust me on this. Cheer up, for pity's sake."

I beam a wide smile but none of my cockney chirpiness can prevent the anguished look that sweeps over his face.

"That's just the point, Phil," he whimpers. "I'm no longer sure how to put my faith in the mighty one, you see."

I take a deep breath. "Come off it, Tom!" I snarl. "What's all this nonsense about losing faith? What happened to the great Chelsea plumber, the man of ingenuity, eh?"

No sooner are the words out of my gob than I realize I've invited him to repeat the usual drivel: how at the time of Queen Victoria's Golden Jubilee, he was happy and confident working on his Kenon trap; how he took pride installing it in Westminster Abbey; how he remembers walking over Tower Bridge towards St. Paul's Cathedral one cold winter morning and felt the world was suddenly too much for him, he could no longer believe in the Guv'nor, let alone in himself; how this despair pursued him relentlessly into the afterlife. He'll bend your ear all day long on the whole bloody saga, if given half the chance.

"It's such a mystery, Phil," he continues. "One moment, you feel cock-a-hoop and then, bob's your uncle, the gates of hell open and this horrible realization sets in that you're on the verge of a meltdown. I just don't understand it."

Now I'm a tough nut, so as I listen to this, I jut out my jaw like Winston bloody Churchill. But, underneath, I've got a marshmallow heart and I can feel it starting to melt.

And I think to myself, "Right we are then! Clearly, what Tom needs is more than Level One treatment. It's time for some Level Two action, a bit of old-fashioned altruism."

I point to the steps leading down from Westminster Bridge to the Embankment. A curled-up body lies in a heap of blankets at the foot of the steps. I say to Tom, "Go and comfort that pitiful creature over there. Go on, sonny. Stop being a whiner and start acting like a winner for a change."

□□□□□

Now, to tell you the truth, I've always enjoyed being a bit of a Samaritan. I'm not partial to the big spectaculars, mind you, like downing doodlebugs or dousing palace fires. That kind of thing is definitely not my cup of tea. A plumber of modest and unassuming ambitions I was in my day, and that's how I like to keep it in the spirit world. Pipes, faucets, escutcheons—the universe of plumbing thrilled me from the early years of my life. Old King Charlie was proclaiming an age of expansion and newfound wealth, and I was chuffed. But who should come along and seize the moment with his oh-so-fancy plans for St. Paul's Cathedral? Christopher bloody Wren, that's who. Of course, Wrennie got all the glory while I carried on doing my duties as a simple plumber, performing honest work underground, out of sight and out of mind.

Chances are you don't know it, but I was the one who installed a revolutionary system of pumps for bringing water from the Thames to a central conduit under Westminster Abbey. Two hundred years later, it was Tom Crapper's turn to continue the good work. He designed a radical system of sewage disposal using a Kenon trap made of gunmetal valves and brass screw caps. Thanks to Tom, Queen Victoria was able to celebrate her Golden Jubilee with all the latest conveniences and hygienic comforts. Yet what did the two of us get for our honest labors? Cobblers, that's all. Not even a simple plaque in our honor.

That's why it chokes me to see Tom losing his way in the afterlife. And that's why it's up to me to fix him. Here he is, poking around the bedraggled figure, all sixes and sevens. I can hear him muttering, "What's the point of this spirit helping business? What on earth am I doing here?"

I realize the time has come to launch into some Level Three treatment: The Big Story.

"Come on, Tom! Follow me." I pull him across Parliament Square towards Westminster Abbey.

"Where are we going?" he asks.

I reply, "To unlock a vital secret of the universe, mate. To realize your potential, once and for all."

We slip through the main entrance to the Abbey, glide past a huddle of tourists at the Tomb of the Unknown Warrior, and proceed down the nave. We shimmy through the ticket barrier to the Royal Chapels in the north transept. Other spirit helpers, from all walks of life, are floating around. But none can match the shiny glow that radiates from yours truly nor match the gravity of my task. We arrive at the Chapel of Edward the Confessor, the very heart and soul of the Abbey.

"Here we are, Tom! This is where my secret lies!" I point to the Coronation Chair. "Right here, where every King and Queen of England has been crowned for the last thousand years. Regard this spot well!" I let Tom soak in the sight and be suitably impressed. "I've waited a long time for this moment, son. Now I'm going to show you what it is that the likes of you and me, simple and honest plumbers, do best in life."

"What would that be, eh?" he whines. "Shoveling shit?"

"No, you daft bugger," I say. "I'm talking about the small things in life with epic significance. The fundamentals."

"The toilet-flush?" He laughs. "Let's face it, Phil. You're not going to convince me that this business of spirit helping belongs to the likes of you and me. We were lowly plumbers, for heaven's sake."

"Ah! That's where you're wrong, boyo. You think us plumbers ain't capable of the occasional miracle, eh? Listen, mate. I'll give you a miracle, all right. One that I was privileged to witness at this very spot over three hundred years ago, at the coronation of William and Mary Stuart."

"Very well, then," says Tom, conceding to my infectious enthusiasm for once. "Proceed with your story if you must."

"Right you are, Tom," I say, chuffed and cheery, and ready to reveal my secret. "The year was 1689. We had been through hard times—Civil War, Olly Cromwell, the Monmouth rebellion, Jacobite uprisings, the whole caboodle. The country was ready for some peace and stability and a union between the Stuarts and the House of Orange seemed to fit the bill. I was at the peak of my plumbing powers. We were well prepared for a double coronation in the Abbey, except for one little detail. We could have used some of your sanitary savvy to solve a particularly odious problem."

A smidge of a smile flickers across Tom's face as if he's already sniffed out the answer but I nip in before he can utter another word.

"Yes, Tom, we had no regulated sewage system in our day. So we relied on chamber pots. Two for every row. Anyhow, the coronation ended up taking twice the normal time because each part of the service had to be repeated, first for the King and then for the good Queen. Well, some of our elderly guests started to obey the call of nature with particular fury, see, and to our horror, loud piddling noises began to echo around the church. It wasn't so much the little belches and farts that was the problem, mind you. No, it was the sound of piss on porcelain."

"Bad combination," Tom says in sympathy.

"The absolute worst, son, I can tell you! You can imagine the look on the face of Bishop Compton who's doing his best to keep a lid on proceedings. He's got feet-shuffling, groans, and farts going off all over the place in his church, not to mention piss on porcelain. Then, to top it all, just as he's getting to the end of his sermon, a bloody great knocking noise erupts from under the Coronation Chair. Right here, in fact!"

I nod in the chair's direction.

"And this is followed by a screech right out of hell. Naturally, panic starts to spread through the Abbey like wildfire. Then, to top it off, the ground starts to shudder under our very feet. 'It's a bloody earthquake,' I think to myself. 'All hell is about to break loose.'"

Tom springs to life. "The Westminster shudder!" he snaps. "Us plumbers know all about that little secret, eh?"

"Well, yes, we do now. But at the time, like everyone else around I was scared stiff. I thought we were done for. We survived the ordeal, as you know. But an inquest began immediately. Some thought the tremor had been an act of God against the Dutch king. Others said it was a Jacobite plot to wrest the crown back to bonny Prince Charles. But I thought to myself, 'Hang on a jiff, I think there's something else going on here.'"

Tom's got that puppy look about him now as if he can't wait to snatch at the metaphorical bone I'm holding in my hand. "I know what happened, Phil," he says, all sweet and smarmy.

But I need to dangle the bone in front of him a bit longer. So I continue my story: "I crept down into the vaults under the Abbey, see, and took a peek at the fittings right below us here." I point to the flagstones where we're standing. "And what do you think I found, eh?"

It's meant as a rhetorical question but Tom can't hold back his enthusiasm any longer.

"Oh, I know what you found, Phil. The check valve on the discharge side of the emission pump had failed to close properly, most likely because there was water overflow in the central conduit. This caused the check valve to slam shut repeatedly which in turn created the conditions for water hammer. That explains the Westminster shudder. It was highly irregular and only happened when there was an unusually heavy supply of water in the piping system."

"Right you are, Tom," I say.

"Did you know that I worked on the same conduit for Queen Victoria's golden jubilee?" the good lad continues. "In fact, the pump was so dilapidated that I had to install a new set of gunmetal valves."

"Right again, Tom! Not to mention your Kenon trap which solved the problem of water running back down the vertical discharge pump. Absolutely brilliant, if you ask me.

Moreover," I say with a whiff of conspiracy in my voice, "I think that we're the only blokes who ever sussed out the true cause of that shudder in the first place."

At this point, you'd expect him to be bowled over by the staggering implications of my story, but old Tom is looking rueful again, like the puppy that's had a taste of the bone and then dropped it in the bloody river in the heat of the moment.

Cautiously, he says, "Come off it, Phil! If I was so indispensable, as you put it, then how come my services to queen and country were overlooked? I mean, it's not as if I was asking to be put on a pedestal like Christopher Wren."

Quick as a snap, I reply: "Ah! But that's the beautiful irony of it all, don't you see? Our lives as plumbers, Tom, have been earthshaking and momentous in their own way. We carry trade secrets as vast and important as the secrets of the universe, mate. Just because we worked underground don't mean we ain't closer to the almighty one, now does it? You can give Christopher Wren his fancy domes and whispering galleries, but at the end of the day what really matters to the Guv'nor, see, happens right under our bloody feet, not pie-high in the sky."

Tom pauses, and then says, "So let me see if I understand this correctly. Am I to be deemed worthy of this spirit helping business on account of my inventing the flush toilet and Kenon trap?"

"Why not?" I say. "Never underestimate the power that us plumbers possess, laddie. We keep the shit moving, after all. And therein lies the moral of my tale."

"But how do I know this coronation story of yours isn't just a load of codswallop?"

"You mean, full of crap? There you have me, Tom! You have to trust me on that score." I indulge in a wicked laugh and I'm tickled pink to see that, after a few moments, Tom finally breaks into a wide-open smile.

We ghost our way through Poet's Corner, then the West Cloister, and exit the Abbey. Outside in the courtyard, by the railings, there's an old woman begging for money. I realize the moment of truth is at hand for Tom so I prod him towards the woman. "Go on. Keep it simple and honest. Nothing flashy at first," I say.

Tom goes over to the woman and gently strokes her on the cheek, then wraps his ethereal body around hers.

"That's the spirit," I say. The woman turns her head skywards. Her eyes look glazed and empty of feeling.

Tom nudges her out of the crouching position, and the three of us start to saunter slowly across Westminster Bridge. She looks down at the river. "Go in peace," Tom whispers to her. Her eyes glisten as she senses the caress of comfort that he provides.

Moments later, we're floating high above the Thames again. All of a sudden, I feel this glow of enormous satisfaction. It's not only because Tom has come through his ultimate test with flying colors, but it's also the thought of us unlikely lads, Tom and Phil, Sadface and Smiler, serving as honorable spirit helpers so long as the Guv'nor has a need for the likes of us.

St. Paul's Cathedral is beneath us now, streaming with the usual tourists. All of a sudden, Tom says, as if on a whim, "Hang on, Phil. Let's pay a quick visit to Mr. Wren's resting place to finish off the morning's good work, eh?"

I beam at him. "Lead on, Tom!"

In less than a jiffy, we're buzzing around Christopher Wren's tombstone in the crypt of the cathedral. *"Sic monumentum requires, circumspice,"* his epitaph reads in big, bold letters.

Alongside, in smaller print, is the translation: *"If you seek his monument, look around you."*

I have to chuckle. "What a bloody joke," I exclaim. "Look around you, Tom. He's nowhere to be seen! He never became a spirit helper, see. Too much worldly ambition, I fancy. That's what this whispering is all about. It's old Wrennie trying to get a word in the Guv'nor's ear. He's still trying to make it to the top, for crying out loud. But he won't get there, I'll warrant. Not enough virtue, plain and simple. He should've stuck to the honest business of plumbing like us! After all, if you look to the heavens for too long, you'll strain your bloody neck."

We share a moment of unashamed gloating. Then I turn to Tom and say, "So, enjoy the last laugh, son, at the expense of our old friend, Christopher bloody Wren!"

No sooner have I said this than I notice a devilish grin sweep over the face of my companion and I realize it's time for us two geezers to scarper and search out other corners of the city where we can continue the Guv'nor's work without too much cock and bull, if you catch my drift.

PART THREE: NOW AND THEN

□□□□□

Sacred Circle

My people sing as they come together in a circle. "Hey-wei-wei-hey-ha." They chant to the rhythm of the great drum on this day of the moon of spring blossoms. They stomp their feet and dance around a gravestone in this place where the wasischus go after they die. Next to the gravestone lies a casket where the bones of my mortal body have been sealed for seven generations. But today, my spirit floats free once again because my people have come to perform their sacred ceremony in my honor.

They have crossed the waters from the Black Hills to this corner that is named Brompton Cemetery in the great city where Mother England lives. They are dressed in red satin jackets and white feathered head-dresses; they are wrapped in blue woolen blankets. The women make a tremolo as my people prepare to carry my bones back to the Black Hills, back to the center of all things. "Uhi-ye-ye-hey-wei."

I will see once again the tall fingers of red rock, the mariposa trees and the cottonwoods. I will hear the call of the meadowlark and the coyote in the early morning. And I will have a vision of my people dancing in a circle, strong and powerful.

□□□□□

The great priest, Eagle Rock, stands in robes of deerskin at the center of the circle. He points with a stick in his hand. He turns to the north, then to the east, then to the south, then to the west. He says: "Look down upon us, gods, spirits, and ancestors. Bless this place. Bless the strangers gathered around us, the kind men and women who delivered us here. And bless the Great Mother, Elizabeth Knight, for returning our beloved ancestor, Long Wolf, to his family."

And he turns to a small white lady dressed in a black robe and brown hat. The wasischu from Bromsgrove steps out of the circle and she speaks: "Thank you all for coming to today's ceremony. I apologize for the drizzle and the dampness. I understand how strange it must seem for you to be here in a cold and wet corner of England, so far away from your homes."

The good lady smiles and my people laugh also. Then she continues: "Ever since I stumbled upon the remains of your ancestor, Long Wolf, in a remote corner of this London cemetery, I knew that it was my responsibility to return him to his people. As you know, he died while touring with Buffalo Bill's Wild West Show. It seems that pneumonia struck him down with swift cruelty. And even though his patron, Mister Bill Cody, liked and admired Long Wolf, the burial was hastily performed and Long Wolf was not granted the funeral rites that a man of his stature deserved. I spent seven years searching for the grave before eventually finding it here, under this poplar tree. Its headstone was, I'm afraid, badly damaged and overgrown with weeds."

She shows her face to the dark sky. Then she says, "I know Long Wolf wishes to be at home with his people, at the foot of his beloved Black Hills. Today's ceremony therefore represents, for me, the fulfillment of a special kind of vision."

□□□□□

The Bromsgrove lady speaks with simple truth. Her words are strong and honest. She has been blessed with the gift of a sacred vision.

I, too, was once granted such a gift.

It was given to me by Wakan Tanka, the Great Spirit, when I was eighteen years old. The Great Spirit's words were whispered into my ear as I lay asleep on the highest rock of Devil's Butte in the Black Hills. For three days and nights, I had gone without food. I had tasted only water and a drop of whiskey, the white man's poison. I was told that the buffalo would return with the wild grasses and that the white man's farms would disappear from the land. I was told that the sacred hoop would return to my people. But the Great Spirit also warned me that I would have to wait a long time for the fulfillment of this vision. The voice went away quickly. I woke and heard a coyote calling in the distance. The sun went down and nightfall spread across the white sky. The air became cold. In the distance, lights flickered on and off. Thousands of buffalo eyes charged towards me.

I decided I must find out why the Great One had given me the vision and when it would come to pass on this earth.

◻◻◻◻◻

In the Greasy Grass Valley of the Big Horn Mountains, I shared a vision with brave warriors from the Blackfeet, Oglala, and Cheyenne.

We cried: "Crazy Horse is coming! Hoka-hey! Hey-hey!"

The valley was dark with dust and smoke. There were shadows all about and there were many cries.

We circled Custer and his men, and put them to death.

I shot a wasischu in the forehead and gained his scalp. In the wind, I heard a voice, "It is a good day to die!" The women were dancing and making the tremolo.

But later, the Black Hills were taken from us. Pine forests were ripped out. Gold was stolen from the hills. The spirit of paha sapa was destroyed. My people, also, were broken.

I went across the big water so that I might learn from the wasischu how to mend the sacred hoop and bring back the vision.

I joined the Wild West Show of Pahuska, Buffalo Bill, and we made many shows in London.

I acted the part of Sitting Bull. I put paint and feathers on me and rode my horse into the great circle of the circus ring. Then Pahuska, dressed in a buckskin coat and long hat, galloped into the circle and made his horse rear up before me. "Sioux, pity us" he cried aloud, and there was great silence in the place. I allowed Pahuska to strike me down with his bare arms. Then I was carried out of the circus ring and the audience screamed with applause. The show was called "Custer's Greatest Achievement."

Pahuska was generous to me. He treated me well and told me he would like to visit my home in the Black Hills. He promised to help me restore the sacred hoop to my people. He said that he, too, had a vision of his people and mine living together in peace. He said that he would like to share this vision with me after we returned across the big water. But first we must finish our last show, he said, which was to honor Grandmother England, the Queen.

I remember the day clearly. Grandmother England arrived in a big, shiny wagon. We danced in a circle for her. She was little and fat and we liked her because she had a kind face. After we danced, she said to us: "I am sixty-seven years old. I have traveled all over the world. But I have never seen such good-looking people as you. If I had my way, I would not let them take you around in a show like this!"

We shook her hand. It was little and soft. We gave a big cheer for her, and then the shiny wagon came and she got into it and went away.

Grandmother England's words gave me hope and strength, but after she left the fever came to me. In the rain and cold, my bones started to ache from sickness. In a dream that lasted many days, I traveled in a cloud. I saw the Black Hills and the center of the world where the spirits would take me. I floated over Pine Ridge and the cloud stopped. I heard frightened people. I saw big pits and silos, rusted trailers and broken-down huts. I saw women and children with cancer scars on their bodies. And then I heard a coyote calling from far away and saw that the coyote's face was my face.

A wasischu doctor looked at me in a frightened way. He said I would soon be dead and Pahuska was going to put me in a box and bury me in a square piece of ground in London.

I knew I could not mend the sacred hoop or bring back the sacred vision during my lifetime.

□□□□□

Now, thanks to the goodness of the Bromsgrove lady, I can finally return to the Black Hills after all these years.

Now, I understand the significance of those words whispered to me by the Great Spirit at Devil's Butte. Like a ripple that grows wider and wider as it moves to the center of a big pond, my vision has taken seven generations to move to the center of all things. By performing one gesture of kindness, the Bromsgrove lady has also created a ripple that will take seven generations to move to the center of the big pond.

My vision is clear. Before me are the valleys and hills of the Great Plains. Gone are the wheat fields, cattle herds, mines, and barbwire fences. Instead, I see buffalo, tall grasses, sagebrush, mesquite trees, and greasewood. In the distance, under a brightly colored arch across the wide-open sky, my people sing as they come together in a circle and carry my body home.

"Hey-wei-wei-hey-ha."

The Night Side of Nature

An Arriflex camera pans across the front façade of a Victorian home in Regent's Park on a damp autumn evening. It tilts towards the sign, "1 Devonshire Terrace," posted on a column in the portico entrance. Then it tracks back to the front window and dollies inside, parting the red silk curtains as it slowly advances into the drawing room. It records a tall grandfather clock, two mahogany bookcases, a cottage piano, and a marble hearthplace above which hangs a large oval-shaped mirror.

The mirror reflects a small group of guests facing a gentleman who is dressed in neatly-pressed dark trousers, white shirt, and red waistcoat. He stands in front of the chimney mantelpiece, framed by the camera's low-angle shot.

The gentleman appears to be Charles Dickens.

The camera slowly zooms in on the gentleman, focusing on his grizzled hair, clipped beard, and chiseled cheeks. It pans across the room, stopping briefly to recognize and establish each of his guests sitting in an orderly semi-circle: John Forster (biographer), Thomas and Jane Carlyle (essayist and spouse), Toby Thanet (travel writer), John Tenniel (book illustrator), and Catherine Crowe (spiritualist).

The camera remains fixed on the latter, noting her reactions as she watches the host with a quizzical frown on her face. Her eyes are held in a steady gaze, and she takes deep, measured breaths. The camera cannot discern whether she is listening closely or ignoring Mr. Dickens as she gives the appearance of looking through him altogether.

It seems that she has just asked the host a question for which he struggles to find an appropriate answer. Mr. Dickens leans one elbow on the mantelpiece and tips a glass of Madeira to his lips. He inspects the bottom of the glass and then looks up again, this time directly at Catherine Crowe.

"I fear I cannot answer this question fully, Mrs. Crowe," he says.

"Cannot or will not?" she replies.

"A little of both, I fancy. The truth is, I simply cannot tell, as yet, how my sister's death will affect my story. Nor do I wish to spoil for you, my honored guests, the wonder and surprise that you might feel upon the reading of it. For I sense that I am in the process of writing the ghastliest story of my life. Indeed, I am slightly afraid of the powers that it excites in me and I cannot tell, frankly, whether these powers are beneficent or evil."

The camera zooms in to catch the slight tremble on the speaker's upper lip, the flicker of his left eyelid, the bead of sweat on his forehead. It watches impassively as he withdraws a handkerchief from his trouser pocket, dabs his face, and sweeps back his hair. He starts to speak again.

"But I can say this! I aim to publish a story that will make my reader's flesh creep, something that speaks to the very nature of the haunted world and those invisible demons that surround us. For I am weary of the burden of Marley's ghost. Yes, I am weary of material phantoms. And this is why I have brought you here tonight."

He pauses to sip once more from his glass, then resumes in a softer voice: "In order to complete my story, I must address a question that continues to trouble me. It is a question that my protagonist must face yet I have struggled to answer for myself."

The camera pulls away to take an establishing shot of the living room. The faces of the guests are now angled intently towards the figure of Mr. Dickens. He takes a deep breath and continues: "I would like to know what haunts us most during these troubled times. What ghastly memory lurks in the nethermost region of our minds, untreated and untended, waiting to resurface at an unbidden opportunity?"

The guests appear reluctant to reply.

"What would it be? I beseech you!" There is an urgency and slight irritation in his voice. "Mrs. Crowe, your book, I believe, conveys many valuable insights into the mysteries of the spirit world. What do you have to say on this matter?"

The camera dollies back to record the reaction of Mrs. Crowe. It observes her in full frame. She wears a loose-fitting black chemise over a dark woolen dress; she sits erectly on her chair; her hands are folded neatly on her lap.

She starts to speak, in earnest, measured tones: "I believe that the world is peopled by spirits. I do not think it appropriate, however, to use the word "haunted" in this particular case. It is overly Manichean. I am interested in reconciling the night and day sides of nature, not placing them in opposition to one another."

As she continues, the camera edges in for a close-up, studying her light-brown eyes, sharply-defined cheekbones, and thick dark hair neatly parted down the middle. She stares ahead impassively as she says, "I welcome your announcement of a new approach to the subject of spirits and ghosts. For I believe, Mr. Dickens, that until now your ideas on the matter have been somewhat mawkish, if you forgive me for saying so. You are correct to identify Marley's ghost as a burden. Indeed, I would go further. It has been a disservice to the science of spiritualism and to our ongoing investigations into the dark side of nature."

"Please continue," implores Mr. Dickens.

"The night side of nature refers to that part of our planet which is turned away from the sun while the other hemisphere bathes in light. And so it is with human nature. I desire to see a conjoining of these two sides. Such an enterprise involves disclosing that part which has been woefully obscured and shadowed."

"Such as?" queries John Forster, entering the discussion with sudden interest.

"Such as those parts that bring about madness and melancholia, or that make us capable of dreadful hallucinations."

A frown sweeps across the face of Mr. Forster. "Surely, Mrs. Crowe, there is something in this dark, supernatural realm you talk of that, for good reason, you would prefer to hide away or keep at arm's length?"

"Please understand," she responds briskly. "I do not feel haunted by anything at all in this world. Rather, I consider myself to be surrounded by invisible wonders. Some people like to call them spirits. Mr. Dickens prefers to call them ghosts. However, I see myself as a spirit of light as well as darkness. The two sides of my nature are inextricably linked."

"My good lady," exclaims Mr. Forster. "Is there not a legitimate reason for such phenomena being obscured, buried, and forgotten? That is to say, isn't it in our best interests that they are simply kept out of sight altogether?"

"You separate the two at your peril," she continues. "If you condemn a spirit or a dreadful memory to the nether regions of your consciousness, they will return later in life as dangerous phenomena, eager to taunt or, indeed, haunt you for the rest of your days."

Mrs. Crowe shifts her attention back to the host. "Take the recent death of Fanny, your sister. Understandably, her sudden departure has gripped you in a powerful way, Mr. Dickens. You seem willing to share your grief in public for which I applaud you. In fact, I believe you invited us here tonight in order that you might discover an appropriate way to express this grief."

The host is quick to respond. "Yes indeed, Mrs. Crowe," he says. "I am inclined to share and celebrate Fanny's zeal for life with you all tonight. But I hope you forgive me if I decline the opportunity to do so, for I cannot yet bring myself around to address the pain of her loss. The sound of her dreadful coughing, as she lay in bed, still overwhelms me with sadness."

A gloomy silence follows, punctuated after several moments by throat-clearing sounds issuing from Thomas Carlyle. He rises to his feet as if he were about to deliver an important parliamentary speech. His burly frame, well-creased face, and energetic eyebrows are accentuated by the camera's close-ups.

"Ah-hem! Dear friends," he commands in a soft Lowland brogue. "If I may be permitted to do so, I would like to add a few thoughts at this juncture. To adapt the words of Karl Marx, a specter afflicts us in the modern era. We are a haunted people and these are spectral times in which we live. But what precisely is this specter that preoccupies us so?'

He swivels his body to the left. "Are we haunted by overripe imaginations, as Mrs. Crowe has argued? With respect, I say this is too fanciful."

He swivels his body to the right. "What of Mr. Marx's notion that we are haunted by the specter of Communism and class revolutions that rage across much of western Europe? Again, I say no! Rather, I believe we are preoccupied by a phenomenon that is closer to home and far more dangerous to the well-being of our souls."

The camera trains itself on his hardworking eyebrows.

"We are haunted by a pitiful specter of the modern man, mechanized and motorized. Dear Charles, if you want a true picture of your haunted man, there you see him: a weary and solitary being with hollow cheek and sunken eye, wanting in intellect and vitality."

It takes a few moments for the camera, like the guests, to realize that Mr. Carlyle has finished his speech and is, in fact, waiting for some kind of approbation. His eyebrows relax. He appears satisfied with his performance yet hesitates to take a seat until Mrs. Carlyle gently tugs at his left sleeve and pulls him back down into his chair, much to the quiet amusement of the other guests.

She, in turn, stands up. She appears to be a modest woman, dressed rather plainly and affected by a nervous smile.

"Thank you, Thomas dear," she says. "I am inclined to disagree with you on this particular issue, not for the first time or the last." There is a sprinkle of laughter from the room.

She continues, "I believe we are haunted by memories, often uncomfortable and unwelcome, that lie unexamined in our minds. If given the chance, these memories transform into phantasms of the imagination."

Her voice grows in conviction as she continues. "Let us be perfectly honest. Who amongst us here has not, at one time or another, awoken at night with a sense that they have been touched by some strange and unexplained phenomenon? The sensation might make a lasting impression or it might vanish with the light of dawn. I have had many such encounters. Indeed, my sleep is often perturbed by the ghostly image of an innocent child."

She glances at her husband, perhaps for moral support, but none is offered.

She continues, "As you all know, Thomas and I have made the decision to remain childless. But what you do not know is the level of grief we endured before and after this decision, nor the guilt I continue to feel for a child who was lost to me ten years ago."

Her voice falters briefly but her body seems to gain in vigor.

"To address Charles's question fully," she continues, "I must tell you how I lost the child that haunts me to this day. I carried her in my womb for seven months, you see. I felt her little bumps and tumbles. Then she was taken away from me after I stumbled on the stairway leading to Thomas' study."

"I did not think too much of the accident at the time, but I was horrified at the words spoken to me by Dr. Harvey a week later: 'If you have this child,' he said, 'I cannot predict what physical or mental deformity it may be born with. That's a risk you would have to take.' He gave me the name and address of a surgeon's office in Camden Town where I went, unattended, on a dark and dreary evening. I cannot begin to describe the dreadful horrors I endured there, nor do I wish to impose them on you at this time. It was as if I had taken a journey to the lower regions of the Underworld. I was immensely grateful to return safely from that hideous place, back to Cheyne Row, and to the settled routine that Thomas and I have managed to establish for ourselves ever since."

She turns to face her host. "Charles, maybe it's a woman's instinct that makes me say this but I believe, along with Mrs. Crowe, that the memory of your sister's death may harm you if it is left unattended. My advice, therefore, is to dive into your memory, dig out your sorrow and deep feeling for her. If you ignore these powerful emotions, then it is you who will become a haunted man."

She reaches out her arm to touch her husband's shoulder, then returns to her seat. Mr. Dickens looks thoughtful. "I see," he mutters.

It is John Forster's turn to speak and lift the gloom. "Mind you," he says in a jovial voice as he springs out of his chair. "It is not like Charles to ignore anything at his peril. Transparent as a window-pane, he is! He has never hidden anything from me, nor from his reading public, I'll warrant."

Mr. Dickens hesitates before motioning to speak again. "Thank you, John. I do have, as it turns out, one particular memory that I have previously shared with some of you before, but I cannot say that I have ever revealed the depth of feeling that goes along with it. Shall I attempt to do so now?"

"Yes, of course, my dear chap," counsels Mr. Forster. "Proceed, I insist. We will hear you out."

"Very well. I was eleven years old at the time. Fanny was thirteen. We had just visited Father at the Marshalsea. As you all know, my father entertained debts of a chronic nature and paid sorely for his financial carelessness. As did everyone else in our family, of course. When Fanny and I left prison that evening, I remember stepping out into the dark alleyway surrounded by high walls. There were no lamps to light our way and the rain was falling steadily on our unprotected heads. We had barely eaten anything all day and my stomach was growling with hunger. It was a Sunday evening and I knew with dread that the next morning I would be returning to work at the blacking warehouse. My sister took me by the arm and I can remember feeling the soft sting of her breath on my wet face as she said, 'Oh Charles! We must look for the music in all this suffering if we are to make something of our lives!'"

There is a commotion in the room caught by the camera as it makes a sudden volte-face. Mr. Carlyle has risen dramatically from his chair. He reaches into his trouser pocket, producing a large handkerchief into which he now blows his nose making a sound like a wet trumpet.

"Yet I cannot go further than this," Mr. Dickens adds as an after-thought. "It is as if I have frozen the moment in my memory and it remains there, static and immovable, disconnected from the events that came before and after."

"That is precisely my point," says Mrs. Crowe. "You must try to probe into this memory and reveal its full implications."

"Yet I insist that I simply cannot do so at this time."

"Come, dear friends," Mr. Forster motions expansively. "Let us allow sleeping dogs to lie. Clearly, Charles is not inclined to pursue this line of inquiry at the present moment. I think we should respect that fact. Now then, let us hear from someone else on the topic at hand, shall we?"

He scans the room and eventually rests on the fresh-faced Toby Thanet. "Ah, Toby! What about you, eh? What do you have to say about this business?"

"I have listened with considerable interest to this evening's conversation," the young man says. "And I marvel at its rich complexity. My philosophy is rather more straightforward. Namely, to have the best of it, you must also remember the worst."

Mr. Dickens nods, as if to make a mental note of the aphorism.

"I must say that I find there is great hope and much despair in the workings of the world. On balance, I believe there is an even keel to life's ups and downs. I agree with Mr. Marx on his theory of the dialectic. But I disagree with him about the direction that human history will take in the future. I have just returned from America where I was witness to an event that both ennobles and threatens humanity more than any recent revolution. I am referring to the discovery of gold on the land of a certain Mr. John Sutter in California. I predict his discovery will bring riches to some but misery and suffering to most. For it will encourage the basest elements of human nature even as it exposes a vast seam of the world's most precious stone. It is a strange paradox, is it not? I submit that such unrestrained greed in our American cousins is the darker side of human nature made material for all to see."

"Yes, Toby," Mr. Dickens agrees. "Even though I was unable to travel beyond the Rocky Mountains on my recent trip to America, I did, nevertheless, take in the Prairies and do not intend any disrespect to that great nation when I say that I still retain the impression of a forlorn landscape spotted with acres of shorn-off tree-stumps. It is a sight you must witness for yourself if you are to believe the abject poverty of the scene. I gather that the hastily constructed gold mines you speak of convey a similarly grim aspect."

"It is difficult to convey the exact grimness of the scene, as you say, Charles," continues Toby Thanet. "But if you care to look at the daguerreotypes of Mr. Basil Hall, recently returned from San Francisco, you will agree with me, I am sure, that they come close to rendering the scene faithfully and naturally."

"On that note," interjects Mr. Forster, "I would like to ask our esteemed illustrator here how he hopes to render, in all faithfulness, those spectral characters from Charles's latest work of fiction? Can he surpass the work of Fox Talbot's box camera or the daguerreotype?"

The camera turns to John Tenniel who sits outside the semicircle of guests. "Well," replies the draughtsman. "You have raised two interesting questions this evening. In order to answer them, I shall adapt a lesson from the actor's craft. The great Charles Kemble once said that in order to express the appropriate emotion in a King Lear or an Iago, he would observe one specific detail, then enhance it, and thus let the particular represent the whole. It might, for example, be a stooped posture in the portrayal of Lear or a curled lip with Iago. And so it is with me and the art of illustration."

"That is commendable," Mr. Forster comments. "I can understand how this holds for the actor, or indeed the illustrator. But I sense a danger when such a theory is applied to my own area of specialty, the art of biography. How can I allow the particular to represent the whole? Surely, if I did so, I would omit the details that constitute the substance of a man's life!"

"True indeed, Mr. Forster. The art of biography that both you and Mr. Carlyle have pioneered continues to enjoy unrivaled success. There is no need for you to make a fundamental shift in the way you practice your craft. Alas, the art of illustrating has been forced to shift dramatically in the last decade as a response to Mr. Fox Talbot's invention. In this day and age, when reality itself can be captured so readily for the viewer, little is left to the imagination. In short, the problem I must overcome is how to compete with the box camera and reclaim the imagination."

"Quite so!" agrees Mr. Forster.

"My solution is to bend reality. Thus, when I compose my portfolio of drawings for Charles's latest story, I shall attempt to emphasize the very essence of his characters' hopes and fears, and I shall do so by exaggerating one small detail in each of them. For example, a pair of thickset eyebrows or a brightly colored waistcoat."

The camera resumes an active interest in Mrs. Crowe who breaks into the conversation with sudden gusto: "You have correctly identified the fundamental flaw with the daguerreotype," she declares. "It can only reflect the surface of those objects that it purports to represent. Yet it cannot probe deeper. And this is the challenge that artists of the modern age must meet. We can and should go deeper! We must penetrate to the very core of human nature!"

A smile returns to the face of Mr. Dickens. "Yes, Mrs. Crowe," he exclaims. "I shall endeavor to heed these wise words of yours." He pauses for dramatic effect. "I truly wish to penetrate further, as you put it. I desire to go deeper into the minds of my characters.

"Indeed, as the evening has worn on," he continues, "I have become increasingly convinced that the supreme test faced by the modern author is how to represent the dark side of nature in equal measure to the light side. Clearly, we must do more to dig out the thoughts and experiences that lie beneath surface appearances. For this reason, I am convinced you will not be disappointed in my latest story. It is to be called 'The Haunted Man.' And tonight, I have acquired invaluable ideas for completing it. For this, I profoundly thank you all."

The host stands tall and triumphant; his size and power are enhanced by a low-angle camera shot. He displays the ease and self-confidence of an accomplished actor. He beams at his guests who now look to him as if awaiting the closing lines of a one-act drama. On cue, Mr. Dickens resumes: "Come, good friends. Let us adjourn to the dining room for a plate of mutton chops. And after supper, we shall be entertained with song and dance by my eldest daughter, Mamie."

The guests file out of the room in pairs, followed by Mr. Dickens who closes the living room door firmly behind him as he exits. The camera observes them as they leave. It lingers for a while, as if contemplating the stillness. It registers animated noises from the dining room, like the sounds of actors who have, moments before, walked off a film set and now babble excitedly as they remove their wigs and costumes. Then it begins to withdraw from the scene, tracking slowly out of the room, past the curtains, through the window, into the cobbled street where it takes a sweeping shot of the house and brightly illuminated scenery.

The cameraman signals to his crew members to stop filming. "Nice job, guys," he says. "Let's take a short break."

He steps down from the camera platform and walks away from the film set, through the studio exit, into the warm embrace of a blue-skied California afternoon.

Eye of Horus

I am Takh, daughter of Pedikhous, doorkeeper of the Great Amun Temple at Karnuk. Chances are, you don't know me unless you've visited the Egyptian rooms in the British Museum of late. But I know one or two things about you. Oh yes, I know about your afternoon cups of tea, milk in first, two lumps of sugar thank you very much, and your greasy fish and chips wrapped in the evening newspaper. I've been around these parts for a while, you know.

Now, by the powers vested in me by the great God Osiris and by the deities that grace this museum wherein my ka and ba reside, I shall attempt to tell a story that scales dizzying heights and plumbs staggering depths. It is a story of soul transmigration, culture collisions, hideous revenge, and the quest for eternal life.

Wozzat?

All right, so I got carried away. I can't help it. I'm a schizo, see. I'll be jabbering on when all of a sudden I get these strange stirrings inside. Before you know it, bob's your uncle, here I am talking in tongues.

O Unem-em-hetep, lord of two lands, I have entered into thee. I have sailed in the boat of Ra from the land of celestial lakes unto the island of Gog.

Actually, I wuz robbed. Back in July 1886, to be precise. That's when Flinders bloody Petrie took it on himself to excavate me and my mates out of our eternal resting ground. Then he had the blooming nerve to ship us over the Seven Seas to room number sixty-three in the British Museum (the one with the mummy collection and swarms of tourists, in case you didn't know). So that's how I ended up in this dump.

Now don't get me wrong, the BM ain't all bad. It's a bit damp and chilly, true, but I've met some nifty geezers here. Take my pal, Thor, for example. He's another one of Petrie's victims, also with a royal chip on his shoulder. He's a decent bloke and a loyal friend, and he knows which side his bread is buttered on, if you catch my drift. Then there's Cleopatra who resides next door in room sixty-four. No, not the Elizabeth Taylor look-alike, I'm sorry to say. You won't find royalty around these parts, that's for sure.

Anyhow, apart from these two sturdy souls, I'm surrounded by a gallery of rogues.

I'm talking about petty thieves, split personalities, restless spirits, corrupt politicians, and murderers. Yes, even murderers.

Hail all ye Gods of the Temple of the Soul, who weigh heaven and hell in balance, and who provide divine justice in abundance.

I know about murderers, all right. I've avenged one or two of them in my time, believe me.

Hail to the Great Takh, daughter of Pedh, the gatekeeper of Amun, first-class avenger!

It was my dad who taught me how to protect myself from the evil eye. By the age of fifteen, I had mastered the principles of geometry and could recite spells from the Book of the Dead. Dad used to tell me: "Keep your face turned to the sun, fair daughter, and you will stay out of the shadows of despair that pervade this land." Little did he know I would be deprived of my native sunshine and forced to spend most of my afterlife in this land of eternal cloud and drizzle. But, to tell the truth, dad's tricks have come in handy more than once since I arrived at the BM, as you will soon find out.

Dad was a bloody good doorkeeper. He knew how to keep an eye on the Gods of the Temple. Unlike Harry over here. I mean, just look at the poor sod, dozing off on his stool, ready to fall flat on his face or his bum at any moment. He probably don't have a clue us sprits exist. He probably don't even care. Still, he wears his uniform and "Attendant" badge with pride, that's clear.

To be fair to Harry, he's caught in a limbo, see. He don't like his job, that's obvious. Who would? Plodding back and forth between rooms with no one to talk to except the occasional chatty tourist. He spends most of his time keeping pesky French school kids from clambering on top of glass cases. Can't say that I particularly fancy the

French either. If it weren't for Napoleon bleeding Bonaparte, we might not have been unearthed in the first place. So don't get me started on that little blighter, or the whole Rosetta Stone fiasco for that matter. The less said about that, the better.

Anyhow, for all I know, Harry don't like living here in England. He's a transplanted foreigner, like me. From Saint Kitts to Kilburn. Not an easy move, I'll warrant.

I confess, I've tried to make life difficult for poor old Harry. It's not his fault. He's just a spoke in the wheel, see, a cog in the bigger machine. I've used my magical powers to stir things up around here. Not that Harry senses anything out of the ordinary is going on, mind you. Like I said, he probably don't even care.

For a long time, I've nurtured a desire to strike back at my captors. Not just Harry. The whole system—Her Majesty's Government, St. George's Cross, 10 Downing Street, Marylebone Cricket Club, everything reeking of Imperial power. I've wanted to put the boot in, inflict a bit of bovver where it really hurts. That's why I decided to become an avenger, first class. What better place to start than my adopted home, the BM?

May I turn aside the great calamities of evil. May I cast the souls of corruption into the fiery Lake of Neserser. May my soul lift itself before Osiris and be deemed pure and sacred.

So that's when I went on a mission. Actually, more than one. 'Cos once you start down that road, there ain't no turning back. I used all the powers learned from Dad: spells, hymns, incantations, the works. Performing acts of sabotage would be an honorable way to right the wrongs of the world, I thought.

It all started out innocent enough. Me and my best mates, Thor and Cleo, decided to fiddle around with Ginger in room sixty-two by fixing her ka and ba.

Do you happen to know about Ginger? She's the tart who was dug up in the Sahara sands over five thousand years ago, gnarled and twisted like a clump of seaweed, but in otherwise decent condition, all things considered. You can see her to this day, lying in state, naked for the whole world to drool over. A shame, really. Still, she's kept a cheerful disposition through it all. There's not an ounce of malice in those brittle bones, I swear. In fact, she seemed positively tickled pink when we snuck into her room and told her of our plan.

"Frankly, my darlings, I don't mind what you do with my blessed body," she said in her sing-songy voice. "I'm a free spirit, after all. Nothing like this has happened to me before. So don't be rough on me."

We gathered around her glass case and started to sing hymns to Osiris, Isis, and Tuat. We sang for the conjoining of Ginger's soul and body in Khert-Neter, the land of paradise. We prayed for her ba and ka to be at rest after their journeys through the underworld and we used the appropriate ceremony from the Book of the Dead to bring this about.

"Observe then, O ye guardians of Heaven, this great soul of Ginger. Even if it would tarry, cause her ba-soul to enter into her spirit-body through the Eye of Horus."

As I continued to recite, I could feel a mysterious energy swirl around us. I inched closer to Ginger's corpse.

"Hands off!" warned Thor. "Remember the edict: no touching allowed!"

But it was too late. I grazed Ginger's hand. Instantly, her left index finger snapped off like a chocolate wafer, and I was left holding it in my hand.

"Oh, great Gods! Sweet Osiris!"

And even though Ginger laughed aloud, obviously not feeling any worse for the wear, we panicked and beat a hasty retreat to room sixty-three, taking the stolen finger with us.

"That's bloody marvelous," Thor complained. "Now look what you've gone and done. You've left Ginger in limbo land and we're stuck with her finger. So much for your brilliant idea!"

"No need to worry about her," I sniveled. "At least she can see the humorous side of it all. But what about this finger? What do we do with this piece of incriminating evidence, eh?"

"Eat it," suggested Cleopatra. "You're jesting, surely."

"No, I'm not. Eat the bloody thing. Swallow it whole. Consume it. Make it disappear into oblivion. Then no one will ever worry about it again."

So I put Ginger's finger in my gob and downed it.

That's when I lost my virginity, as it were. I was no longer pure and unsullied. Inside my ka-body, a bit of a foreigner now floated like a key rattling around in a glass jar.

□□□□□

After this royal cock-up, you'd think we'd be savvy enough to stay away from further shenanigans.

And we did for a while.

That is, until the visit of Tutankhamen, old wonder boy himself. No doubt you can remember the hullabaloo he stirred up during his world tour in '72. Showing off his gold ornaments and gemstones, he bedazzled the public in Paris, Rome, London, New York, and Tokyo. What I didn't anticipate was that he would stir up one or two things in me also.

I knew Tuttie was peeved about his excavation by Howard bleeding Carter. But I hadn't sussed that the lad was also nursing a serious shoulder-chip that kept his ba-spirit thirsting for revenge. That's where King Tut's curse came from, see. And he used it to good effect against Carter's right hand man Lord Carnivore when the poor sod suddenly dropped dead from a mosquito bite. Then, on the same day, all the bloody lights went out in Cairo. Spooky, that.

Of course, like all kids, I was obsessed by the mystery surrounding young Tut's death when the lad was only nineteen years of age. Did he die of some horrid natural disease or was he murdered by some power-hungry nutcase?

One night, as Tutso lay in state in the Great Exhibition Hall of the BM, me and my mates gathered around his gold coffin and he spilled the beans: "It was an act of violence by the traitor, Aye. The villain resides here in your chambers. Seek out his ba and ka and avenge me! Use your training well, my fellow countrymen."

He described the ghastly event in all its gory detail: how Aye, his so-called trusty adviser, snuck into the living quarters of the royal palace and performed the dastardly deed on the sleeping pharaoh. One swift whack to the back of his head, that's all it took. What really put the old tin lid on the whole sordid affair was that this Aye chappie went on to marry Tutsie's widow, the beautiful Ankhesenamen, and then had the blooming nerve to bump her off too!

"But why would he do that?" asked Cleo, innocently.

"So he could claim the royal throne all to himself," Goldenboy replied. "That's what he wanted all along. Undisputed power."

Oh yes, it seemed we had a nasty piece of work in this Aye geezer. What's more, he had been our neighbor in room sixty-four all this time. To tell the truth, I hadn't given much though to him since his arrival. He was a loner, preferring to be known simply as "Aye, civil servant of the eighteenth dynasty," just like it said on the label of his glass case. I did not imagine he had at one time aspired to become the most powerful man in the world. It bothered me now to think how, despite his infamous deed, he was saved at the Weighing of the Heart and then admitted to the Field of Reeds. What's worse, his ba-soul and ka-body had been allowed to roam around the hallowed hallways of the BM with all the privileges accorded to a member of the royal family.

I knew a worthy project when I saw one. I said to my mates, "Right we are then! Time to roll up our sleeves. Let's get to work!"

I planned to avenge Tutankhamen's murder by blocking the Eye of Horus engraved on Aye's coffin. My goal was to prevent his ba-soul and ka-body from ever wandering freely again. They would be trapped for eternity in a dark casket in an obscure corner of room sixty-four. By performing this task, I felt I would be taking revenge not only against Aye, but also against the greedy lusts of ambitious upstarts in ancient Egypt, not to mention power-hungry imperialists everywhere. Oh yes, I would teach them all.

The three of us—Thor, Cleo, and me—performed the sacred rituals with perfect precision.

"Hail, thou God Anin! Hail, thou God Pehreri! Hail to thee, Osiris, Lord of Eternity, King of the Gods! Thou art the Great Chief, the Creator of Right and Truth throughout the world. Bestow upon me the power to give bodily action to my righteous anger against those who have crossed over the line of incorrect behavior. And grant me the strength to fight daily against Set and the Ways of Darkness.

"O ye guardians of Heaven, cover the Eye of this wicked soul so that its inhabitant may never again return to its abode. Restore peace and honor to this place."

"This one's for you, Tuts!" I screamed, as we reached the climax of our operation. And so it was done. With these incantations, we plugged the Eye of Horus, trapping Aye's ba and ka inside the casket until kingdom come.

Oh yes, I felt chuffed, all right. After all, we had set in motion the machinery that would atone for evil and restore justice in the world. Tut-boy had even said that if we successfully performed this noble deed, he could forever lay to rest his curse. His spirit could now return home in a state of blissful equanimity.

I was on a power trip and hungry for something bigger and better. The mother of all acts of revenge would be next. I wanted to strike at something in the BM that symbolized the heart of Englishness. So, as my next target, I chose the Lindow Man, Boadicea's bog-boy, ancient Britain's sole survivor.

"Oh, come off it!" protested Cleo. "Now this is going too far. What are you going to do with the poor sod? Make him disappear, like Ginger's finger?"

I considered her point and answered boldly, "I will arouse his ba-soul and then have him help us fight the good fight."

Frankly, I didn't have a plan. I simply wanted to stick the boot in against the Lindow Man as the symbol of the whole bloody establishment.

"Now look here, Thakh," Thor joined in. "We didn't mind working with you on the Aye project. Eye for an eye, tooth for a tooth. That's one thing, lassie. That was in the family, as it were. But this new idea about smashing the symbols of imperialism, the establishment, whatnot. Why, Cleo and I just don't go along with it. We think you're barking up the wrong tree. Why can't you just let sleeping dogs lie? I mean, what do you expect to get out of this anyhow?"

"Revenge!" I shot back. "A feather in the cap for cultural purity. A defiant blow in our ongoing battle for repatriation."

"It can't be done. Impossible! Look at you. Look at me. We're hybrids in a museum. We're floaters. Stuck in the middle. Neither here nor there. There ain't no going back!"

This riled me. "You're a race traitor, Thor," I sputtered. "You've lost your spunk, your ka, your ba. You've been fraternizing too much with London yobbos."

Cleo piped in: "Listen Thakh. I think Thor has got a point. I've always felt our motto should be 'adapt and survive.' I just don't understand how this act of revenge is going to make any difference whatsoever."

"Right then! I'm on my own, eh? Fair enough. I know on which side my bread is buttered." I turned my back and ghosted over to the west wing.

If I was going solo, then so be it. I could a fine job without anyone else's help. I would turn up the heat. This was going to be a major spectacular.

So I prepared for the ceremony with extra special care and attention. I wanted to make sure nothing would go wrong. I would resurrect the ba-soul and ka-body of the ancient Cheshire lad and then use his revived energies as a weapon against the Great Enemy. Well, something along those lines, at any rate. I trembled with excitement as I recited the words from the Liturgy of Resurrection:

"Hail, O ye who make perfect souls to enter into the House of Osiris. Let this Creature of Lindow, he of the smashed skull and garroted esophagus, rise again in spirit. May his ba and ka enter boldly into the hallways of our museum. I offer sepulchral meals, incense, and unguents so that he may be delivered into the afterlife. Let us rejoice now, as his soul and spirit are reunited to come fully into voice."

It was intoxicating.

I ended my invocation and within seconds heard a croaky voice.

"Corblimey mate! Wazgoin' on, eh?" It was the resurrected Lindo Man, no doubt about it.

I answered him in a reassuring voice, "How are you feeling, old chap?"

"Bit woozy, like. Know whattamean? Flippin' 'enry, a bloomin' steamroller creamed me in the noggin!'" He looked around. "Who art? Where amst? How long have I been aslumber, then, eh? One day? One year? One sun orbit? What planetary conjunction is this?"

Now that his ka-body was reanimated, his smashed skull and twisted torso didn't look quite so grotesque. But it worried me that the geezer sounded like a drunken idiot.

I said, "I've brought you back to consciousness using special incantations from the Book of the Dead."

"Yajestin'? Whafor in 'eaven's name?"

I was beginning to doubt whether, at this rate, I would be able to manipulate the imbecile so as to execute my plan of revenge against the museum. But it was too late to turn back. Now that I had revived his ka, it was the turn of his ba.

I created an Eye of Horus on his body with a gentle incision and soothing rubs. "'Ere, that tickles, darlin'. Git yer bleedin' 'ands offa me!"

Undeterred, I continued chanting.

"Grant that this body may return to spirit-life from its state of impurity and decay. Hold not its ba-soul in captivity forever. Release it now so that it may travel freely on the open road to the Fields of Everlasting Peace."

Half way through my recitation, my worst fears came true. His ba got stuck in the middle of the Eye. In a panic, I poked around further in his torso and started to pull.

"Please!" I cried out to the gods. "Not now! Not this time!"

The plea went unheard. Bog-boy's ba came whizzing out of that hole and launched into me like an express train hurtling into a tunnel.

And you think that was bad enough? Lindow Man's soul became part of me.

It was a culture collision of the highest order. Or another royal cock-up, depending on how you look at it.

That's when I became a true hybrid, a pedigree-flavored mélange. And that's how come I talk like this, see. I can't help it. I open my mouth and god only knows what comes streaming out. A bit of cockney mixed with high Egyptian and the occasional scouser's slang thrown in for good measure.

I tried explaining the situation to Thor and Cleo but bog-boy kept interfering. "Kicked in the 'ead, I wuz. By the bloody Druids, see. Oy! Nuffin' to laff about, youse two."

"Perhaps it'll teach you to forgive and forget," sniggered Thor. "After all, you're not going to right every wrong in the world now, are you?"

"Easier said than done," I replied, finally getting something resembling my old voice back. "But, there again, you might have a point. Maybe I should give this forgiveness stuff a try. Maybe I should just enjoy being a half-caste, a mongrel, my ka and ba floating between two lands like a ship at sea."

But in case you think I've copped out altogether and lost my cultural bearings, don't write me off just yet. I've still not forgotten that I hail from the great civilization of the Nile Valley. That's why, at night, after the hordes of tourists have departed, and Harry's tucked inside his bed somewhere in north London, I regularly recite my prayers, just as Dad instructed me: *"Let my tomb, and my friends who are upon this earth, flourish in the land of Britannia. May we set sail in the Boat of Millions of Years towards Sekhet-Aarn, the Field of Reeds, and may we safely arrive at the Nome of Maati, the Place of Eternal Truth."*

I'll never lose hope of returning home, no matter what Lindow Man might have to say about the matter.

London Spirits

High atop the London Eye, luminous Boadicea sits in a translucent capsule. Down below, on the banks of the Thames, ethereal spirits mix invisibly with boozy celebrants of a more corporeal nature. A new millennium is dawning and London's inhabitants, past and present, are on hand to participate in the Great Games.

On the South Bank, between Westminster Bridge and the Royal Festival Hall, supporters of The Plebs huddle together in their outfits of baggy black trousers and shapeless red pullovers. They are souls deemed in their living day to have blundered somehow. But it is not for them to reason why they find themselves, at this moment, on the wrong side of history's seemingly arbitrary selection process. They know, with stoic resignation, that they are the underdogs, the dispossessed, the downtrodden.

On the opposite side of the river supporters of The Lucky Few are spread out between Big Ben and Somerset House. Bedecked in white flannel trousers and shiny blue blazers, they paint a picture of privilege and refinement. These fortunate souls have carried into the afterlife a particular talent or gift which they wear with unashamed self-confidence.

And in the middle of the river, on a ghostly barge, stand six players, three selected from either side. Team members from The Lucky Few perform their calisthenic preparations with professional ease while The Plebs labor with amateurish uncertainty. Both teams eye each other with a mixture of scorn and suspicion.

Surveying the scene, Queen Boadicea rises from her seat on the Great Wheel, inhales the midnight air deeply, and then bellows forth in a voice of megaphonic proportions: "My fellow London spirits!"

A roar of approval issues from the jostling crowd, followed by a football chant from an unruly quartet of sophomoric spirits on the

South Bank, "Ooh-ah-Can-ton-a!"

The Mistress of Ceremonies looks on with condescending amusement. "Thank you, gentlemen, for that kind gesture! Now, shall we begin?"

She pauses briefly, her enormous frame filling the night sky like an ashy cloud from a volcanic eruption. Then she resumes in a regal tone: "We are gathered here on this auspicious occasion to celebrate the dawning of a New Millennium. However, before I officially consecrate tonight's games, allow me to pay tribute to this great city from an unashamedly patriotic perspective."

Boadicea raises her arms in a mock-heroic gesture, not unlike that of an overzealous Shakespearean actor, then plunges into her recital: "O fog-shrouded city, drizzle-dazzled town, metropolis of mud and thick materialism, what can I, your guiding spirit, say that has not already been said about these two thousand years of history? What common thread can I find in your stories? What is the shape of your historical narrative?"

For a moment, there is a stirring in the crowd, a collective puzzlement, "'Cor blimey, mate, what's the old lady on about, eh?"

Undeterred, Boadicea continues: "Fellow Londoners, I have journeyed with you through cycles of birth, growth, decline, death, and rebirth. I fought against the Roman invaders. I witnessed plagues and great fires. I watched buzz bombs and doodlebugs light up the winter sky. I observed the construction of architectural wonders from Westminster Abbey to Battersea power station. Throughout it all, I have marveled at your collective effort to build here, on this swampy plot of land named Londinium, a place that for a brief moment in human history would become the center of the world's attention, a vast imperial power, a place for faraway cultures to dream about and mythologize."

She takes a deep breath and then, assuming the stentorian timbre of Winston Churchill, continues: "And I have been seduced by the names and events that have shaped the narrative of the Great Wen: Magna Carta, Thomas More, Dick Whittington, Queen Victoria, the Blitz, the Festival of Britain, pomp and circumstance, John Bull, pork pies, baked beans, Typhoo Tea ..."

Sporadic drunken cheers greet the mention of a staple beverage.

"Yes, yes, I know," she concedes with a wink of an eye. "We all love our little indulgences now and again, don't we? But seriously, my friends, it seems to me as if, throughout this historical journey, we Londoners have adopted the ways of a slightly awkward teenage boy—rough, rude, crass, cocky, not particularly elegant, unruly, lewd, lusty, yet loveable in a peculiar way.

"Yes, loveable!" she emphasizes. "There is a laddish innocence in how we go about our daily business, whether it's a nip down to the pub or scoffing an over starched meat pie. At times, I see this spirit embodied in a choirboy: high-collared, rouge-cheeked, and falsetto-voiced. At other times, I see it more as an urchin: cockney-smart and naughty, yet graced with a kind of Dickensian sincerity."

Queen Boadicea rears up mightily, and continues: "Now, let me get to the heart of the matter. I believe there is more of the feminine principle, the creative anima, which waits to be discovered and articulated around us. For starters, we might celebrate this spirit in the statues and monuments of our ancestors. How about poets, philosophers, and artists along Whitehall instead of field marshals, viceroys, and governor-generals? How about that, eh?"

She folds her arms on her chest and beams a satisfied smile at her spirited audience. "My fellow Londoners, I see vast potential around me as we gather to celebrate the new millennium. I see the churlish yobbo and the animated poetess vying for the coveted title of cool Britannia. And I believe this will be the shaping dynamic of our future. A powerful creativity is about to be unleashed amongst the dead and the living of our city. That is what I—Boadicea, Warrior Queen of the Iceni—have watched and waited for during my extended reign as spiritual guardian of this great city."

The crowd is hushed, like a football stadium moments before the chanting of the national anthem. Then Boadicea lifts her arms to the sky and commands: "Now rise up, you spirits! Rise up, I say!"

Turning to the six contestants on the river barge, she commands, "Whosoever can answer the following riddle shall win a place by my side on this Wheel of Eternal Salvation. But be warned! Finding the answer will require a mixture of wisdom and sporting prowess. Now, my friends, are you ready to begin the Great Games?"

The uproarious cheers that greet Boadicea's inquiry are not unlike those that welcome a seasoned pop star's arrival on stage.

"Very well then, players," she continues. "You must show me, with actions as well as shrewd insights, what sport we Britons are best known for around the world? The rules are quite simple. Each team shall take it in turn to make three attempts. Now, who is bold enough to go first?"

The first to step out of the players' barge is the bearded and burly W. G. Grace representing The Lucky Few. With bat in hand, he hooks a shiny red leather ball for a boundary.

"It is cricket, madam," he asserts with calm confidence. Polite applause ripples from a pavilion of smartly dressed supporters assembled fantastically behind him.

"Not so," comes the immediate judgment from Boadicea on high. "As a world power, England's mettle has been tested of late and she has lost. Her innings is over, you might say. She has been hit for six. Next batter up please."

From the opposing team emerges a portly man announcing himself as Arthur Compton, a carpenter from Darlington. "Tiddlywinks, that's the ticket," he says nervously into a microphone hanging from the sky. And then he demonstrates with dexterity the art of the double-flip on an oversized red counter that sails gracefully over the heads of admiring onlookers before landing with a plop in the middle of the river.

"Alas, no!" retorts the mistress of ceremonies. "I find this a tedious, small-minded game befitting a small-island mentality. To the back of the line you go."

Boisterous cheers accompany the next contender, one of The Lucky Few, as he enters the contest. The sprightly Stanley Matthews, sporting number seven on his shimmering blue shirt, starts to dribble a football around the river buoys with swerving skill and ease as if he is skating on ice. He stops, looks up, and proclaims: "It's the beautiful game, ma'am. Football, futebol, soccer. That's the answer to your question. That's why we're loved and admired all over the world."

"Wrong again!" comes the reply from above. "Not enough tactical acumen in the national team! Too much reliance on the predictable long-ball, I'm afraid."

Hoots of derision emanate from a scattering of hooligans who have by now spilled onto the river. "Gerroff! Bollocks! What a load of rubbish!"

But the shouts die down as Sid Jones, a rotund, friendly-looking man, looking every inch a Pleb, steps up to hurl a feathered dart with pinpoint accuracy at a sign on the middle arch of Westminster Bridge. "Pub darts, luv! That's the game we're best at, ain't it?"

"Close to the bullseye, Mr. Jones, but no cigar! Sorry, old chap."

Both teams look despondent as the midnight hour approaches. The Lucky Few offer a last contender—a strapping hulk of a man who introduces himself as Roger Penrose. He gathers an oval-shaped ball into his hands and punts it clear across the river. The he turns cockily to the Mistress of Ceremonies and offers his answer: "As every public schoolboy knows all too well, the sport we have given the world, for which we are universally praised, is rugby union. Not for nothing did we spend countless hours after school slogging in the slashing rain and rolling in the mud of our playing fields. That's where we learned to acquire honor and virtue, to be men of dignity and integrity."

Boadicea remains unimpressed. "All well and good, and highly admirable," she replies with sarcasm. "But the might and power of the Lions have consistently been overwhelmed by Kiwis and Wallabies, I notice."

The river scene hushes as the final Pleb, a waif of a girl, floats across the river to the foot of the Ferris wheel, looks up, and says: "Begging your pardon, miss, but I do not have a sport to offer. For, in truth, I think that as a sporting nation we're right crap! The only thing we Brits are good at is losing with honor."

Boadicea is gently amused. "So, child, do you have an answer to give me? Pray continue if you do."

"Excuse me, miss, but I think the answer is 'fair play.' It is the art of being able to keep a straight bat. Of keeping your head about you when all those around are losing theirs on a sticky wicket. It is playing by the book. See, I've done all this, miss. I have played by the book. Yet it never got me very far, to be honest. I've been a constant loser at the game of life. I suppose that's what I do best, like most of us on this island. But as long as we give it our best shot, the full hundred percent, there's no shame in our failure, now is there? We're really good at being honorable losers, see."

There are roars of approval from supporters assembled on the South Bank; agitated protestations from the opposite side. Boadicea pauses dramatically, then exclaims: "Why, yes, of course! This is a splendid response. For, surely, the correct answer to the riddle is, indeed, the sport of 'fair play.' Young girl, you have earned a place for yourself on this Wheel of Good Fortune. First-class seat! And, prey, what is your name?"

"Monica Smith from Durham, if you please, miss. A coal miner's daughter, I was. Died from tuberculosis when I was young, begging your pardon. But I've always been a good girl. I've tried to do my best. I never had a fair shot during my short life, see."

"Yes, indeed, child. I am pleased to say that your virtues will finally be rewarded. Come, young Monica. Rise to the occasion. Join me here on this seat atop the wheel."

At Boadicea's bidding, the coal miner's daughter from Durham floats to the top of the Eye and takes her place alongside the Mistress of Ceremonies.

Howls of indignation spew from certain boys-in-blue on the North Bank. A toffee-nosed official steps forward and appeals to the great authority on high: "Now, hang on a jiffy! She's stolen our terms of reference, don't you see? We invented the notion of 'fair play' on the fields of Harrow and Eton, after all. That's what the British Empire was built on. Stiff upper lip and all that. You can't take away that achievement from us. It's preposterous. Why, it's simply not cricket."

Boadicea grins and hurls back her riposte: "Ha! I'm afraid you've been hoisted by your own petard, Sir Oswald. Hard cheese, eh what?" And to the strain of "I Vow To Thee My Country," the London Eye begins a slow rotation as fireworks start to light up the sky and mortals jostle unknowingly with immortals on both riverbanks.

Of course, there are those who insist, to this day, that at the dawn of the new millennium when the Eye was intended to make its inaugural turn, it remained stubbornly motionless because of a mechanical failure. However, mortal eyes would not have noticed the wheel's otherworldly movement, nor could they have observed the two spirits inside their cozy capsule who were, by now, locked together in an animated embrace that would last an entire revolution.

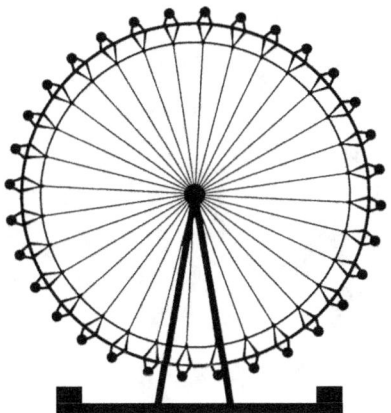